Shortest Day
Longest Night

Stories and Poems
from
The Solstice Shorts Festival
2015 & 2016

Edited by
Cherry Potts

ARACHNE PRESS

First published in UK 2016 by Arachne Press Limited
100 Grierson Road, London SE23 1NX
www.arachnepress.com
© Arachne Press 2016
ISBNs
Print: 978-1-909208-28-5
Mobi/Kindle 978-1-909208-30-8
ePub 978-1-909208-29-2
Edited by Cherry Potts. The moral rights of the authors have been asserted.

Printed on wood-free paper in the UK by TJ International, Padstow.
Supported using public funding by the National Lottery through Arts Council England.

Individual Copyright

CONTENTS

Shortest Day Stories

Shortest Day Poems

Shortest Day Lyrics

Longest Night Poems

Longest Night Stories

SHORTEST DAY

A Ten-Point Temporal Sample of a Hundred-Thousand Unanswerable Questions
Sarah Evans

07:00

I wake to questions: Who am I? What was I just dreaming?

Is that really the time? How can it be day when it's still so frigging dark? What would happen if I failed to get up?

I summon willpower and lurch into the shrivellingly cold air, asking myself – yet again – why don't I set the heating to come on earlier?

The cold is just diversion though, isn't it, from deeper issues: Why am I alone? Why didn't you return my call? Then again, why should you?

None of which helps with the pressing decisions of the moment: Shower first or breakfast? Muesli or pop-tart? Cranberry juice or black coffee? Radio 4 or Magic FM? Try ringing you again, or not?

08:00

Does the wind have to be so bloody cold? How come the traffic lights never work in my favour? That guy honking his horn, can't he just give me a break? The stained reds and oranges of sunrise are beautiful, so why do they depress me?

What possible excuse does the barrier have for rejecting my ticket? Rear lights and an empty platform: why are these so desolating? Couldn't the train have been late this once when it would actually have been helpful? I could use the time to ring you, only what would I say that I haven't already said a hundred, a thousand times?

I've waited longer than anyone else, so how the hell do I end up standing? Why can't they put on longer trains? How come other people's coffee smells so enticing? When we finally emerge from the blackness of this tunnel, will you finally have texted me back?

09:00

Why do I wish I was anywhere but here? What is my task for the day? Which of those ringing lines should I pick up? Am I better getting stuck in, then grabbing coffee later, or the other way and how is it that after all these months I don't have an answer to that?

Did I ever even have a chance?

10:00

Why am I making all these calls and not the one I want?

Hello, is that Ms Winterton? Could I have a few moments of your time? Would it be alright if I run through a few questions?

The woman's expletives ring in my ear and how is it people feel it's OK to be so eff-ing rude when I'm only doing my eff-ing job?

What is it that you are doing right now?

11:00

Are you branding loyal? How would you rate the quality? And who gives a shit?

Is Market Research Interviewer the world's most boring job? What does that say about me? Is this why you left?

What is your household income? Would you recommend to a friend? What improvements would you like to see?

How can I persuade you to change your mind? Please, please tell me: who should I become?

Are you interested in learning more about your sleep? Is your bedroom dark? Do you currently share your bed?

Is there someone else and if so what does she have that I don't? Would sending another text seem less desperate than another unanswered call? How can I persuade you to reply?

12:00

Is it too early for lunch? Why do I buy overpriced sandwiches and then not enjoy them? My screensaver loops through the company mission, vision, objectives, and why does that crap drain me of all motivation? My personal goal is just to get through each day, but shouldn't I be more ambitious? Why do they never fix the flickering strip-light above my desk? How did mayonnaise end up smeared over my keyboard? Why do they add so much garlic? That time you said my breath stank from last night's curry, do you know how truly regretful I am?

13:00

How long do you spend every day on social media? How many Facebook friends do you have? On Twitter does the number you follow outnumber your followers or vice-versa?

Would my supervisor notice if I checked social media for the hundred-thousandth time? Why did you stop following me?

Do people answer surveys honestly? If I made the answers up, would anyone detect it? That thing you said which made my heart sing, did I misunderstand, or did you only mean it at the time, or not mean it at all? Why did I believe the good things, but not the bad?

14:00

How can the shortest day spent here feel so endless, while the longest day spent with you passed in minutes? I yearn to fast-forward through the hours, but aren't I just wishing my life away?

What do you use your computer for? How many hours do you spend on the internet? What are the three most common topics amongst your friends?

I think of you constantly and how is it that I'm managing to function while memory eats me alive?

15:00

How important is each of these statements to you? What would you say are your two favourite ice-cream flavours? How do you feel about low-fat products?

How is it that I feel so much and you so little? How can two people have such a fundamentally different view of the same relationship? You told me that you still care, so how come you still left?

16:00

The windows fill with the glow of sun-sink colour and it's one hour to go and why do I look forward to returning home, when the flat is full of nothing but your absence?

Hello, is that Mr Lewis? Mrs Sharp? Mr Maclean?

Am I wasting my life and who cares, given it all comes to nothing in the end?

Why? How come?

Why does all of it, every damned thing, mean so little and yet matter so much?

Please answer my calls.

Please help me understand.

Hello? Hello? Are you there?

Without Index
CB Droege

'We must find the answer,' the scholar said to the linguist, 'or this could be humanity's last day.'

'I know the stakes,' the linguist replied, 'and you just made me lose my place.'

They sat in silence for a time among the towers of books and scrolls and clay tablets and bundles of loose parchment tied up with twine, on all sides, so that the walls could barely be seen – they were surrounded by the wisdom of the ancients. Only the two of them could hope to decipher it all.

'This is hopeless,' the linguist said, 'there is nothing here that will save us.'

'Humanity survived this event once before,' the scholar said, holding a finger to her place in a crumbling scroll, 'surely someone wrote of how it was done.'

With renewed vigour, they continued their search.

Morning light began to pour in through the high, cobweb-dimmed windows of the room. The linguist sneezed, and dust which was once a roll of parchment scattered across the room in a rolling cloud.

'Sorry,' he said, 'I hope that wasn't the one we needed.'

'The world shall not be undone by a sneeze,' the scholar said, barely looking up. 'Keep reading.'

The dust settled, and quiet descended again as they continued their work. The morning light moved across the wall as scrolls were re-rolled and set aside, as tablets were stacked in face-down piles in corners.

'I think I've found it,' the linguist said, knocking over a stack of bound and illuminated sheaves in his rush to consult.

'This is not it,' the scholar replied, 'but perhaps we are close.'

A bright light shone redly through the high windows of the room, burning away the cobwebs from the window and bringing the smell of burnt dust into the close quarters. Both looked up. For a moment they were blinded.

'The time has come sooner than we thought it would,' the lingusit said, face in hands. 'Perhaps we were not the right ones for the job.'

'We were the only ones,' the scholar said, and humanity's shortest day came to a close, and its longest night began.

In the Gloaming
David Mathews

A woman in a cottage doorway, cosy in an old fur against the cold, needle, threads and linen in her hands, a kitchen dark behind her.

'Will you do me one of your eagles?' the letter from the south had said, 'by Christmas?' They are impatient folk in Edinburgh.

The last one, Lucia had decided. No more till the days grow lighter.

Look at a golden eagle in the life, and it is the eye that grabs you, an eye intelligent and alien. Lucia holds her work close. Four black stitches make the pupil, seven of yellow the iris. One more stitch, white, will make the eye seem to catch the light, a single stitch to render the exact degree of wildness. Where to place it? One thread too far left, and the bird would be tame. A thread too far the other side and the bird would come across as altogether deranged.

The stitch goes in. How is it?

Lucia's eyes sting, and need to rest on something green and distant, but winter and her failing sight leach the colour from the houses and fields round about. All the same, she relaxes, her thoughts going to a picture postcard from her grandparents' village – uncle Renzo's panetteria, fixed by Kodak in the same glorious monochrome she sees now. Blindness is a sod; it creeps up on you in many ways.

'Good morning, Lucia. You're well wrapped up I see. Is that your eagle you have in your hand?' Willie always has a word for Lucia.

'I just sew the eye. He look bad-tempered.'

Willie peers at Lucia's work, sucks his teeth, nods. 'That's your eagle for you. Will you get him done the day?'

'Only if the light improve, Willie. Where the sun when I need it?'

The old man laughs, and waves his hat to Lucia and to the midday clouds, urging them to part.

One Hogmanay Willie kissed her, a solemn kiss, a nice enough kiss, but he did not excite her.

So many uses for a mouth. Kissing, biting, sucking, licking, wooing and loving, giving voice to anger, joy, grief and terror. Lucia puts two fingers to her lips. One finger is calloused from the needle, hard like the scar on her Angus's lip that surprised her the first time, and was still there at the last. Oh...

The beak of an eagle is not like a man's mouth. When the postie brings a letter from Lucia's sister, he touches the soft threads that depict the hooked and terrible instrument. 'You would not wish to be a rabbit in the open, or a wee lamb with that thing about, would you,' says Andrew. 'That beak's a nightmare.' He shivers as he makes to leave. 'Keep warm, Lucia.'

She finds it hard to stitch inside the cottage. Outdoors is better for her eyes than her brightest lamps, but today is tough. Sunrise was before nine, but you could barely tell, the light having been slow to make its way earthwards through dark clouds – and not much quicker since, despite Willie's exhortation.

'The sun comes via Glasgow,' they say hereabouts.

Embroidery mimics feathers so well that, as she works on a half stretched wing, Lucia feels the bird's strength. Even so, how can such feathers bear an eagle, heavy as a new-born baby, higher and higher until it is just a dot? The world is full of wonders.

On she goes with the wing. After that she will be done.

Lucia hears Jessie singing on her way home from school.

'Jessie, patatina, can you give Nonna a help?' She has a bribe. 'Yesterday I have make struffoli.'

The girl sorts threads too similar in tone for Lucia to tell apart, and leaves with a bag of the balls of sweet dough to share with her sisters. Lucia is 'Nonna' to half the village children.

When Angus Ross left the navy and returned to his native northeast with his slip of a girl from Italy, he and she were celebrities. They seduced their neighbours into a love of pasta, some highly un-Scottish types of bread, garlic, olives, wine, grappa and the siesta. Their noisy lovemaking at all hours scandalised the street – deliciously.

Forty years on, there are a few folk who snub Lucia, punishing her for dead Angus's diligence in the matter of collecting rents and debts when times were hard. They envy her artistic skill with venom. 'The macaroni witch' they call her.

To most of the village, however, she is a treasure, an exotic, still so very Italian in her speech and tastes.

'That's your eagle for you.' Willie had said of the stern bird. Over the years, Angus's eye had become an eagle's, distrustful of the tenants, and treating even his wife as inclined to deceit. Only once in a while would his eyes soften and twinkle rather than pierce her. Lucia blesses Angus's memory for those moments of fun, when she would tease him for his foibles, and he would praise her wisdom, and kiss her.

Forgiveness for Angus's later years came after he turned his eye on himself, and after his eye, his gun.

The glow from neighbouring houses mocks the little daylight that remains. Lucia is defeated, the wing feathers she knows as coverts still to be finished. She shuts her eyes to ease their ache, unsure what she regrets most, the dullness of the day or its brevity.

She returns to the kitchen, and sits in the dark, the better to chat to her lost Angus, share their bright days in Naples and Capri, taste his mouth, and watch, always watch his eagle eye.

Hunt and Pray
Katy Darby

A lot of people these days say they don't believe in gods. It seems to be a modern fad, whenever we are now (twentieth century, twenty-first? I lose track) to dismiss the old deities in favour of the new. Allah and Osiris and Kali have been around a lot longer than internet and self-help and L. Ron Hubbard, but perhaps that's why some worshippers become bored and stop praying, then stop believing altogether. Even though us old-timers are good at godding, a deity can't go on without believers and so yes, some of us are dead now. Where do dead gods go, you wonder? Do gods have an afterlife? I wonder too, but I sure as Hades don't want to find out.

There used to be seven of us up here at the frozen top of the world, where the days and nights are seasons long. It got a little crowded sometimes, with disputes over territory and jurisdiction, but basically we all rubbed along for millennia. In the good times we were praised and in the bad times, prayed to: that's how it works being a god, there's really no downside. Except when people stop believing in you altogether, or abandon you for a new deity. Except when you disappear.

I was talking to an oilman in a bar in Qaanaaq once and he said he was surprised the Inuit had seven gods of the hunt. I said, I'm surprised your language has only one word for snow. There's hunting in the sea and hunting on land, I told him, like I was spelling it out for a kid; there's hunting alone and hunting as a tribe. There's net-fishing and spear-fishing and whale and caribou and shark hunting, what, you want one god for all that? Would you use the same weapon to hunt a caribou and a whale?

I guess not, he said, but I could tell he was more into pussyhunting than any other kind. He was lucky he didn't try it on with my sisters Arnapkapfaaluk or Senga: both would have killed him without a second thought. It wouldn't have looked like a divine execution, of course, just a heart attack, but we huntresses take no prisoners. What would be the point?

The others always said I was a soft touch, the weak one: not just goddess of the hunt, but medicine and fertility too. (That's why I flirt with out-of-towners when the chance arises). My whole family looked down on me, back then; especially Tekkeitsertok. Well, who's master of caribou now, Tek? Nobody, that's who, because animals can't pray and nobody else believes in you any more.

Poor Tek. He never listened. Neither did the others. People will always want children, need medicine, I would protest mildly as they lorded it over me, Nerrivik, Nujalik, Arnakuagsak and the rest. They scoffed, they laughed. People will always need the hunt! they said. What, one day humans will stop eating fish, catching seal? You're crazy, Pinga! Get over yourself.

They didn't listen, and now they're gone, swallowed by McDonalds and Pot Noodles and microwave Kraft dinners. I'm the one who guides dead souls to the afterlife (on top of everything else) so if anyone should know where the others went, it's me; but I don't. They just weren't there one day. We didn't exactly meet up regularly: like most families, we have some conflict issues, but somehow I'd always thought they'd be around. Despite knowing, remembering, what happened to Isis and Cotytto and Bast, Su Ka and Quetzalcoatl and all the others.

Who? Exactly.

Nerrivik and me are the only ones left now, and only because she's still the patron goddess of fishermen, whether Inuit, Canadian or whatever. They may not know they're praying to her when they hit a swell or hunker through a storm, teeth gritted, lashed by salt-ice; but they do. She's old, though, and tired: she sees the long night approaching but doesn't want to fight it.

Ma, I say to her, we've got to do something: the humans strive for survival, why shouldn't we? But she just sighs in that enormous, empty way, like the sea against the night-shore, and says, Pinga, a mother should not outlive her children. The shortest day will come soon. Wherever your brother and sisters have gone, let me join them.

They're nowhere! I tell her. There's nothing! Don't you get it? The afterlife is for people, Mama! All we have is life. She shakes her head and closes her greyblue eyes. There's ice behind them, creeping cold.

But I won't go quietly. I won't lie down for the darkness. I've got quite a spread of duties: birth, death, hunting and health. It would be weird if the goddess of all of that didn't want to struggle for life; the last breath of air, the last drop of blood, whether the blood of hunter or prey. I'm the youngest and I deserve to live as long as any other god, that's how I see it. I am the last and I will claim my birthright. Other gods have done it. Other gods are stronger now than they have ever been. Why not me?

So I'm on the hunt. The hunt for followers, for worshippers, for believers. But why should I stick to the well-trodden paths and the old sea-lanes, follow the ancient tracks in the snow? Why stay in Greenland at all? There's hardly anyone there, and the population that does exist prays to me anyway, for babies and healing, and a smooth passage into the long night after the shortest day. But I want more. This huntress is hungry. For light. For power. For life.

What happens when the food source dries up, or moves? The hunters follow. And what gods feed on is belief. I need to reach out to a lot of new believers. And I'm willing to travel. So, people of London, next time you're ill or injured; next time you screw your husband and wish for a baby, I'm the one you pray to. Not Allah, not Buddha, not St Michael or the Virgin. Me:

Pinga. I may be foreign, I may be different, but I'm all about customer service. Try me out: see what I can do. What have you got to lose?

The Cutty Wren
David Steward

21st to 22nd December, 1916

Today, the light failed by mid-afternoon. We've been marching under cover of darkness since regrouping at Lapugnoy, where we stocked up with ammunition. The weather's been deteriorating, hard rain during the day and freezing cold at night. We grease our feet beneath our socks but still my toes are numb.

The dark is close and safe. Brunny said, 'I reckon I must've slept sitting up in the saddle. You en't going any faster than a hodmedod, and all you can hear is the ratticking of the limber and them old chains a-chinkling. That's easy to doze off.'

He's carved a tiny bird out of wood from a broken cart. It's a tradition in Suffolk, he says, to hunt the cutty wren at Yuletide. In ancient times she dwelt in the underworld and country people killed her to end the winter. He keeps his carving in the top pocket of his tunic. He'd let the wren live, he says.

I wish I could carry a place with me in the way he does: I'd cling to it for distraction. There's no comfort in the bricks and cobbles of Whitechapel. In my memory, the little damp rooms are just a succession of temporary lodgings. I filled my days walking among strangers in their streets, withdrawing each evening, as if to lock the gates on a ghetto.

Last night, we struggled to climb a hill, which necessitated a stop to fumble in the bitter cold, screwing cogs into the horses' shoes, to fit drag ropes and haul on the limbers, then wait at the top for the animals to get their wind back. Exhausted, Brunny sat on the frosted grass and drew each arm in turn across his face. When he sucked in air, I realised that he was sobbing quietly.

'We're through the worst of this year.' I placed a hand on his shoulder. 'The light's coming.'

'That's nothing we can look forward to,' he said. 'Just more time for the snipers to get us while we're sitting up like hares.'

Groundhog Day Suicides
Jamie Der Wahls

It had been so real. It had been – alarmingly real. But in the end, it was just a wish-fulfillment dream, like Dorothy and Oz.

She sighed, a long, bitter exhale. But this didn't change anything. She threw the covers off and called work, just like she had in the dream.

'I'm not feeling well,' she told them. It wasn't a lie. She hadn't felt well in months.

Really, she thought, the dream was pretty damned useful. She knew exactly where the traffic jam was. And when she drove to the store to get ammo, she knew which cashier to choose.

She drove home again. She sat on the couch and phoned her sister again, to say goodbye. She knew she was getting the answering machine, and this time, it didn't throw her.

She smiled, just a little, to herself. She drew the circle again, the same one that she'd done in her dream. It had been a little joke, one she'd intended as a gift.

She sat down on the hard wooden floor, in the centre of the charcoal circle. She scrawled the same intricate diagrams that she'd drawn last time, the ones she'd found after thirty seconds with Google image search.

As she ran a finger along the gun, she smiled. The world was... not, strictly speaking, fun. To be blunt, a lot of it was boring, a lot of the time. 'Programmer kills herself' would not have been news. But if the cops find someone dead in the middle of a black ritualistic circle, candles burning low, blood seeping into the grooves she'd carved in the floor...

Why, she just might make someone else's life more interesting.

She knew that the diagram was bullshit; she literally found it by Googling 'ominous rune'. But some cops would get that strange terrifying sting of childlike wonder, that sudden feeling of being over a yawning chasm where reality itself seems torn, when they realise that the world as they know it is insufficient to contain reality.

'There are more things in heaven and earth, Horatio...' she muttered to herself.

She lifted the gun to her head. She had researched how to do this. She held it a few inches behind her temple. None of that 'became a vegetable' bullshit.

'Take two,' she said. And fired.

*

It had been so real. It had been... alarmingly real. But in the end, it was just a...

...what? Wait.

No, that hypothesis was losing ground.

She drove to the store and mouthed along to the conversations that the shoppers were having. She called in to work and knew verbatim what her boss was going to say. She hastily drew the circle, and then, thinking a little more, drew it *very carefully*.

'No way,' she said, raising the gun to her head.

*

It had been so real. It had...

It *was* real.

'No way,' she whispered.

And then...

'Oh my god. This is so *hackable*!'

Her face split into a grin. She was unlikely to be the first person to discover this... why would that circle just *happen* to work? No, it was probably...

It was probably an easter egg, left behind. Someone else had discovered this, and, well, really, what was the risk of leaving the diagram out there? No one would believe it, and even then, no one would test it if they believed it. It took a lot to kill yourself. She knew.

But someone else had found this... an accident? Maybe. Or maybe it was something fun, like *an ancient and secret cabal that ruled the world*! Oh, she'd be seeking *them* out soon.

Her mind was buzzing. She would never mess up a conversation again. She knew the winning lottery numbers. She could loop as much as she needed and see the future. She could spend all of her money in a day and do it all over again the next day. The same day.

She laughed then, wild and free, like she hadn't since she was a child. She had found magic after all.

Happy Hour
Lee Nash

It's not so strange.

In Sydney you can buy an *AB* pizza – that's *AB* for abortion. If that's to make a point or just be crass, I don't know. Here the message isn't subtle, but they pull it off with class. It's Friday and we order *Tourist Kill, Finless Shark, Orphan Orangutan* because we ran out of time to save the whales but don't want to drown our conscience.

The pianist wears a panda suit and the barman wears a tee which reads, 'Adopt a Vaquita'. He winks at us and fills his shaker, topping up the chrome with vodka shots and healthy juice, the *Vaquita* sloshing happily around the bar. A waitress speaks to us in tiger. She brings us two *Blind Elephants* in glasses ringed with coloured ice, creamy like liquid ivory. I wonder at the name. To get their tusks they take it all – the eyes, the face.

It's cooler now – the days are getting shorter, we're into autumn. The rhinos take to the floor and dance and no one finds them foolish.

You think we're odd, sad eco-weirdos, nothing but a bunch of dodos. I say we're doing *something*, say, what are *you* going to do? Are you going to do it *now*?

You say you have time, that even the shortest day has just as many hours.

Most of them are dark, I think, but I don't want to offend. I offer to buy you a drink.

Will you have a *Passenger Pigeon*? A *Baiji White Dolphin*?

Mercury
Pippa Gladhill

I lost concentration one millisecond, the net hissed over me and down I hurtled, crash bang. Me, winged Mercury, go-to-guy, messenger to the gods, light as an ice sliver, quicker than the bolt sizzling from the miraculous blue; me, who nips round the universe, guiding losers to the underworld, meddling with the ways things are, unsettling and raising the dead, chucking 'em back into the stream of life – with their rackety clackety bones – one minute I'm hurtling through the twilight, and next, flapping and struggling, captured, cast in stone, and plonked on the roof of the mouldering heap of stately building that is Dyrham Park.

'Mr Jon Vost,' I said, in my raspy voice, 'paint my twirly stick gold. If it's not gold it has no power and I can't escape the dead weight of this cold stone you've trapped me in. I can't move.' But he ignored me.

'Oi, you can't leave me like this. If I'm stuck here, then so are all who have to get to the underworld. *Stop*,' I shouted, 'wait, paint my stick gold so I can fly away – Mr Get Lost, *listen*,' but he carried on humming and tap, tap, tap, with his chisel, as if he couldn't hear me.

So, here I am opposite this stupid, stone eagle with his dead eye, angry glare and clunky wings. We stand frozen, opposite sides of the roof, like we're about to pace out a duel. Silence. The stars come out. The wind blows. A fox skulks about in the shadows.

'Hey, get you,' Eagle says.

I try shuffling my feet to loosen them. I try waving my stick around.

'I'm not stuck,' I say through gritted teeth. 'I'll be off soon.'

'How do you work that one out?'

'On the day of lowest ebb, the khufu ship, the tipping moment, the point when the sun's rays at the particular flat angle, will shine on my stick and turn it to gold, then ... I'm off.'

'I have absolutely no idea what you're talking about,' says Eagle. 'Look, there's a badger.'

'I can't see it.'

'You're facing the wrong way.'

I try craning my neck round, but it's rock solid, what with all the staring up at my outstretched arm and the stoniness of my life. 'I can't turn my head.'

I wait. The days do their thing, one after the other, like days do, never quite the same and never quite different. I fizz with impatience, until, at last, the short day, yes, the tipping point, the moment of reversal of the ebbing sun; but, what is this? There is no blooming, ebbing sun to cast its low angled light onto my stick and turn it to gold. No sun, no light, just a grey, drizzly drizzle.

'Hey, man, thought you were off today,' says Eagle.

'Yeah, but I need the rebirth of the sun god, the year as reborn –'

' – too bad, we got fog.'

'Ah, but look, never mind that, rescue at hand, we got men, putting up scaffolding. They've come to chip me out of the stone and set me free. I'll be off, lighter than the sunbeams dancing on the sparkling waves, quieter than the dew settling on the morning grass, I'll be quicker than the –'

' – spare me,' snaps Eagle. 'Where will you go?'

'Look out there. What do you see?'

'People aimlessly looking at things.'

'The undead you mean – doomed to search endlessly round stately homes for the underworld because I've been stuck up here and not able to guide them.'

'Oh do me a favour,' says Eagle.

'So, first, I'd take 'em to the underworld, then I'd bring back the logjam of reprieved souls, then nip to the Aegean, the bluest sea the whole world over, dip my winged feet in the water, and from there, a skip and a hop to Mount Olympus, check out the scene, who's hanging out. Where would you go, Eagle?'

'I'd go and sit in the branch of that Scots pine over there,' Eagle says.

'That's not far away.'

'Who needs far away?'

'Far away is always better than here. Listen, Eagle, when I set you free, you can go anywhere you like in the whole wide world.'

'I like that tree,' Eagle says. He sounds obstinate.

There's more hammering and banging, shouting and yelling. The scaffolding is up.

'Oh ye gods,' I say. 'I can't wait to get away from this stupidity.'

A guy in a yellow hat walks my way. He pats me on my knee. He pats me, son of Zeus, winged messenger to the gods, on my knee.

'Keep your hands to yourself,' I rumble in my throat.

'Now what's happening?' Eagle asks.

'He's coming back with a chisel, any day soon,' I say.

I think about my freedom returning. I tingle all over, in a slow, stone like way, with excitement. Then yellow-hat man returns. No chisel. Just big tins of paint. *Paint?*

After it's all over I say 'Cream coloured masonry paint? They're mad. They have no idea, they don't know what they're doing.' My winged feet, my heart, feel heavy.

'Hey,' says Eagle. 'Far away isn't always best. Tell me about the sea. What's the sea?'

I look out over Dyrham park, the big oaks, the deer nibbling the grass, the buzzard showing off above. And I think: there will be another chance. After a lot more of these days, coming as they do, one after the other, there will be the moment again, the tipping point, the rebirth of light, with the khufu ship, low angled beams on my curly stick which will turn gold and off I'll zip, higher than that scraggy buzzard.

'The sea – I'll describe it. How long you got?' I hear eagle shake his stone feathers. He doesn't answer for a while.

'A long time,' he says.

Deliver Me
Rosalind Stopps

Doncaster Station. Dark. Wind whistling. Food wrappers snapping. Doncaster, the station where nothing good happens. Things get lost. Lost tickets, lost hats, lost hopes, lost loves.

'They need to work on their image,' I say to Miles, 'ask people to write down little stories about things that have happened here, so they can make a display.'

Listen to yourself Kathleen, I think, could you be any more boring? No wonder he's tired of you.

'Sorry,' I say. 'Once a teacher, always a teacher.'

I attempt a gay laugh, the old-fashioned meaning of gay. It doesn't sound right.

'Death, disease, pestilence,' says Miles, 'stories of man's inhumanity to man.'

It's grim but he's joining in, speaking as if we're having a real conversation, just the two of us. It's been so long I almost clap, but I don't. I stand there, rooted to the spot by the closed coffee kiosk, waiting for a prompt.

'There's probably been some nice things here as well,' I say. 'People meeting up for the first time, or setting off for the seaside, or going to start a new job.'

I am thinking that perhaps people have fallen in love here or mended broken marriages but I look around and I have to admit it's not likely. There's only one other person I can see and he's curled like a foetus in winter wrapping, asleep on a bench.

Miles stares intently at the floor by his feet as if there might be a camouflaged trapdoor hidden under the pigeon shit. He puts one hand on the wall. He has never had good balance.

'Hey,' I say, 'maybe the floor will open up and there will be a whole other world underneath. With Oompa Loompas and bubbling cauldrons and everything.'

I'm trying too hard. I can hear a faint whiff of hysteria in my voice. He sniffs in that way he has. I know it would be better if I could just keep quiet. We could still turn this around, I want to say. We could make it into a funny story. Or a heart-warming story, at least.

'Guess where we were when we decided to stay together,' I would say. 'Go on, guess. Doncaster Station, can you believe it? On the shortest day of the year, too.'

I'd leave a pause then, wait for whoever was listening to say, 'what?!' or, 'Really?!' and I'd be ready. I'd jump back in and I'd say, 'Do you know, if Miles hadn't left his hat on the train when we were on our way to Hull for my uncle's funeral we would probably have gone ahead with the divorce.'

We've got a chance, I can feel it.

'Maybe it will turn out well, you losing your hat,' I say.

Miles kicks the wall like a thwarted fifteen-year-old.

'Fucking shithole,' he says. 'Typical day out with you and your fucking family.'

The injustice nearly knocks me over. I start to cry and the cold is good camouflage. It isn't my uncle's fault that he died in December. And it isn't my fault that Miles has lost his hat.

'I've lost things myself often enough,' I say.

It's true, I have, right here, dashing for the Hull connection. The voice on the tannoy always reminds you to take your belongings with you but umbrellas, hats, wives, it's easy to leave them behind.

'I'm sorry about your hat,' I say. 'I'll try to get you another one when we're back in London.'

'I don't fucking want another one,' he says, more like ten years old now than fifteen, 'and I don't want you. I want the hat I left here this morning on the way up when you tried to rush me off the train. We're going to wait here until the lost property opens even if we have to wait all night.'

I get nervous when he gets like this. I get nervous and I talk rubbish. Gibbering, Miles calls it. It winds him up and I know that but I still can't stop.

'It might be warmer in the waiting room,' I say. 'Look, there's a heater.'

'Fucking longest night of the year on fucking Doncaster station,' Miles says.

That's when I have my unusually daring idea.

'Are you sure?' I say. 'It looks quite cosy in there.'

'Fucking cosy,' he says.

A globule of spit flies out and lands on the platform.

'What the fuck are you talking about, you stupid woman?'

Stupid woman. It's better than some things I've been called. I want to smile but even though he looks as if he isn't taking any notice of me, I know he is. I have to be careful.

'I'm worried you'll get cold, without your hat,' I say.

I place my foot nonchalantly on the tiny piece of spit as if I am covering evidence.

I listen to the announcements while he rants and kicks at whatever he can find.

'Are you ok?' I ask. If I was a talking doll with three different things to say on a loop, that would be one of them.

'Of course I'm not,' he says, 'I want my fucking hat back.'

Petulant now, more like a five-year-old. We're moving backwards, I think.

When it happens it's so quick that I'm not even sure of the running order. I think it's this.

'Oh gosh,' I say, peering onto the rails.

I do not say that I see his hat on the railway line. Just, 'Oh gosh.' I'd heard the announcement that the next train wasn't stopping at Doncaster, that it was going straight through.

'What?' Miles says, 'What?' and he's peering over the edge

and he doesn't notice but I hear it coming and it's only a small nudge but it's enough, he's never had good balance and he wheels his arms and his own trajectory does the rest. He topples but he doesn't even fall on to the line because the train is there instead flinging him up and out and suddenly there are pieces of him flying around, a leg and an arm, everything but a hat.

After today the days will be getting longer, I think. The thought makes me smile.

Darkest Night
Polly Hall

Sister, please listen to me. Your life depends on what I will share with you. I am your true friend and secret guide. We are in this together, so everything I say to you is sacred, I bring you hope.

Firstly, believe in your beauty and power, honour it as a branch reveres its berries, it is yours to keep or bestow on others as you choose.

I am proud of your strength. You hold a great burden, but with a lightness that does not crush you, you do not complain.

You are sacred earth, sacred fire, sacred water, sacred air.

Sister, listen to me now. Let us go deeper, let us go to the depths that are unspeakable. I feel a thousand fists pounding at your chest. You are as strong and as powerful as the sun. By shining your light, you attract the night creatures, the shadows that stoop and blink into the light of your body. They bathe in it, but give you no recognition; they believe you are there for their pleasure, at their disposal.

No, sister, *No! No! No!* Burn those shadows with your inner fire. Burn them so that their flesh peels and chars, burn them so that their skin melts onto stony ground. Send them to their ashy grave and let the winds of heaven blast them to the four corners of the earth.

Do not rest now. I know, you are tired; but we have so much to do this night. You must leave these tricksters. They have no concept of the rebirth of the sun. It is beyond them. They will expect you to be their mother. Do not mother them. You are your own mother. Draw up your power and awaken your cells. Set your bar high. You are perfect and should never be ensnared.

Dear sister, let us raise our eyes to the mountain tops, let us fly on the powerful winds of change. Let us be carried, above the clouds, the birds, the oceans, the savannahs, the canyons and the beasts of this earth. Spread your glorious wings and inhale deeply the heady juniper and cleansing rosemary of the season. I am with you at all times and in all space.

Feel the warmth and the heartbeat of mother earth, a drum resounding in your chest. Feel its greatness rise, each part of your body filled with midwinter wisdom, ignite the fire inside you, let it reach out to the corners of your mind, radiating heat, intensifying and purifying.

Become the fire, become the fire, become the fire and let yourself taste the red, white, gold and green.

Let it go. Let your entire burden go and the new you will find meaning in all things. Sing the beauty of your shadow as you emerge from the darkest night.

The Ornery Orrery
Roger W. Hecht

'This orrery is stuck!' cried Machiavelli. 'The planets don't align. Now, how will I predict the rise and fall of kings, the comings and goings of plagues, and on which horse God wills I should place my ducats?'

Leonardo, with an eye toward the mechanical, squinted at the marvellous machine: its wheels and gorgeously engraved discs, its metal spheres perched on sticks. He tried its brass gears, tightened and loosened screws, worried at the crank. He recognized the problem at once.

'Fool,' he cried, popping the flat-topped cap off the Florentine's head. 'Don't you see? This machine can't even exist! We live in a geocentric universe. This heliocentric universe won't be confirmed for a hundred and fifty years!'

He relabelled the celestial objects and the truth became perfectly clear. 'Besides, your dripping candle jammed it here.'

He flicked a plug of wax off with his knife, turned the crank, and set the future in motion. The wheels turned freely. Planets spun their orbits. Eclipses came and went. Fruits tumbled from their branches. Princes became obsolete while the sun stayed firmly in place.

'I see,' the master statesman murmured, astounded, as his world fell to ruins before his eyes, like clockwork.

Cut Short
Sarah James

Damn, late again! I fidget with my car keys, a reflex action, as I'm tempted to bail on lunch. Sundays should be the longest day – lazy sex, coffee in bed, newspapers, novels, Netflix, not getting dressed until three, if at all… Ever since university, I've made it my personal quest to stretch these twenty-four hours of the weekend as far as humanly possible. But not today.

It's three months now since I last made it to a family dinner – my absence noted, effort expected. Before I even leave my flat, I feel the day contract to the size of childhood Sundays: the shortest day of the week, the one with gritted teeth, church and my gran.

When I get to Mum and Dad's, Gran is already there, watching Mum colander the carrots, stir the gravy, transfer serving dishes to the dining table… Gran's lips are tauter than telegraph wires, and I know she will have been stood like that ever since she arrived, probably around eleven, but maybe even earlier.

Though I've succeeded in missing the preparations this time, I know every minute of the scene, memorised from first school, through my teens and college: Mum's white knuckles tight on her sharpest knife, as she chops veg, meat, the next few hours of her life. With each cut, the day of rest gets shorter. Afterwards, she washes the board until each fragment, each drop of blood has drained away, then pivots back to my gran's rigid face. Every movement, word and breath in the house is subdued by Gran's presence in the kitchen – silently critiquing, helping with nothing – right up to the final stiff goodbye…

But not this Sunday! As Mum hands Dad the carving knife,

its steel blade glistens, and my day pulls back against its enforced shortness. I jolt myself from the ritual to take our plates from the oven and press their warmness towards my gran instead of Mum.

Gran blinks, doesn't move for a second, then accepts the towelled stack and turns towards the dining room. As she turns, at the corner of Gran's lips, a twitch – the trace of something that's almost a smile. When she holds up her plate for Dad to fill, Gran grips the porcelain a little looser, then passes the gravy to Mum.

The End of Everything
Liam Hogan

People assume I get up at dawn. Sometimes, when the lamps flicker on, a glimmer of false light that precedes the real thing by at least an hour, I wish that were true.

But at this, my favourite time of the year, it is not such a hardship. It's during the summer months that I start to feel sleep-deprived; the days of work too long, the nights of sleep far too short.

Whatever the season, I eat a simple breakfast; a high energy slow release sort of thing, before I descend to the stables. It's still quiet, but at my approach there's a faint snicker as one or more of the horses stir. It's usually Bronte, a subterranean rumble to her breathing. But by the time I slide back the bolts, all four are awake; expectant.

They're eager to be up and running. For them, the long winter nights are no great boon. To each his, or her, own, I say.

'Good morning, Aethiops,' I softly call. 'Good morning, Sterope.' I lower a sack of oats from my shoulder. The same oats I ate earlier, though my four horses, two male, two female, the males taking the trace, the females the yoke – my four horses prefer their oats raw. Eous nuzzles at me, trying to make me spill more than his fair share, but I'm careful that none of them gets more than any other. They must pull equally; they must pull together. Things go awry when they don't and this is not the day and age for things to go awry. Maybe once I could get away with it, but now, any indiscretion would be quickly spotted and cause the greatest of turmoil. My route is circumscribed.

It is good that my horses are so well behaved. The most

beautiful horses ever to have lived, I proudly claim; sleek and powerful, as they have to be for their unusual load. Intelligent, too. Far too intelligent, sometimes.

After they have fed, I take care to brush each of their coats, to comb through their thick manes. I run blunt hands over their fine limbs, making sure they are and remain in good health. Occasionally, and fortunately rarely, one turns lame and I need to borrow a replacement. Those are not generally good days. Even as I do my work I worry about leaving a poorly horse behind, untended and alone.

I check my watch. It was a gift, a railway man's pocket watch, the numbers large and easy to read, the knob for adjusting the time protected from accidental knocks. It is the same device that allowed the British railway system to run on time and on schedule – for a while, at least, and it serves me the same purpose.

Before I had it, before it was invented, no-one would notice if I was a few minutes late, or a few minutes early. But those times are past. My comings and goings are written down months, years in advance.

Today is the winter solstice: the shortest day of the year. The mares are restless, brimming with too much energy. I slow my brushing, doing my best to calm them.

Once each has had equal treatment, I turn my attention to their tack; to the bridles and straps, the reins and the trace. No saddles; these four horses pull a chariot.

It is the chariot, of course, and not I, that brings the dawn.

I leave hitching it to the last minute. Once it is attached my horses will have no choice but to pull away from it, to protect themselves from its fierce heat and light, even at this time of year.

As we ride out of the stables and take to the skies I breathe in the cold air. You'd have thought a sun god would be used to the heat, would miss it even, but I always enjoy that first crisp gulp, a taste of the last of the night. Today it is scented by wood smoke and heady with the forthcoming festivities, the ones that should really have taken place last night, as they did in olden times, at the very turn of the year.

And then we're climbing, soaring, and I must pay close attention to my route.

Even so, and as I may have mentioned, this is my favourite time of the year.

It isn't simply because I savour the extra time in bed and most definitely not because I do not enjoy my work, my allotted task. It is because, at this time of the year we fly so much closer to the ground, barely clearing the trees even at noon. And so I get to watch, as each of you goes about your carefree business, safe in the certain knowledge that I can't possibly exist.

Safer still in that I will never forsake my sworn duty, for to do so, even for a single day, would mean the end of everything you know.

Brother and Sister
Tom McKay

Pit pat – his school shoes make the sound of *pit pat* – and the strap of his bag makes his knuckles white as he runs *pit pat* towards the sky. He is going home. The peak of the old classroom falls away behind him sharply – concrete – and he imagines the everlasting shoulder of the earth beneath him waiting. He is also remembering an image of a man from the afternoon's history lesson – with rough hands – striding giant across the earth. And from deep within the earth the squelch of his shoes picks out the footprints of bound toes and shadows of families encased within the peat.

He remembers about a girl found crystallised with woven hair and the teeth still in her mouth, and his feet beat out the memories as he runs. He imagines the space beneath him – miles deep – and he thinks of the girl's parents among those watching as she sank beneath the soil. He sees her father's hand clasped on the feathery bog plants as his insides sunk down with her. He makes a strange fantasy that he has no father and no mother, and that his little sister is buried deep in the belly of the ground. He makes another fantasy that he is running to an imaginary grown-up brother's house and there he will find a sitting room with saucers and radiators and televisions – and mugs of brown tea with bowls of white sugar.

*

She is looking out of the sitting room window into the garden. It has stopped raining and the light is fading. The air is still a bit blurred – but despite this the grass is shining green – and all the fences around the garden and the houses behind are fuzzed though a squint of grey. The room itself is dark because the greyness is lightless, and she can almost feel the shape of herself against the window. She remembers an ancient holiday, when she was smaller, too small to be herself – but just the right size to be dragged by her arm along streets with angles leading down and signposts heading off.

Now the sense of someone watching has left. In the dream he was behind her all the time, clattering darkly. He had limbs, but they were sort of mixed together in an effort to walk about. The dream man had a body that no longer worked – because all his limbs were like a chopped-up photograph. The shadow man behind the back fence had gone as well, she hoped that he had gone home – and the grass was shining green. She noticed that there was only one other thing out in the garden that refused to be grey; a small black and white thing under the hedge that must've wanted to be seen. There were always dirty feathers in the garden – but it wasn't them this time. The cat had been missing for three days. At first she had cried and they had looked all over the house, in the cellar, in all the boxes. Finally they looked in the cupboard with the plates, because once when it was a kitten, they had found it there, sitting in a dish waiting to be discovered. It wasn't anywhere. She had cried and felt in the pit of her stomach the feeling of panic – a reaching sense of the bottom falling out.

Now she is looking out the sitting room window for her brother to get home from school; she is thinking that he'll know what to do.

In the Blind

Katy Darby

This is Cera Mulcahy, transmitting in the blind. Station 156, population twenty-three, duration seven months two weeks five days. We can't hear anything down here but we're reaching out to whoever can hear us, reaching out in the blind.

OK, first things first. If you're listening, if you're trying to find us, Station 156, it's the blast bunker under the old Town Hall. You can't miss it – well, not till it got razed to the ground along with everything else. It was an ugly beast, Sixties concrete from back when they'd let you knock anything down and build anything else on top of it. I suppose those days are back again; the first part, anyway.

I'm tired. Tremors all last night, 2300 to 0400, maybe 0500. I kept waking up in panic, half-sitting to check on the girls and then remembering. Listening in the green darkness. Falling back asleep. We haven't seen daylight in about six months now. The generator fuel's running low so electricity's rationed. Our 'days' are getting shorter and the nights longer. One day soon, the night won't end. Dan and I have been on eighteen consecutive night watches now, which is why he's sitting next to me, head thrown back, snoring like a chainsaw, and I'm transmitting to you, whoever you are, out there. If you are out there.

Dan says we should maintain radio silence, that if we make any noise over the ether we'll attract them, but I think we're way beyond that now. If you're listening you probably know what happened, but just in case there's someone out there this didn't touch, someone who's looking around at the total destruction and wondering *WTF?* let me explain our situation.

They appeared nine months ago and it took them maybe nine weeks to drive every remaining living human underground. I say they; we have no idea what they are. We have no idea who they are, what they want, how they think, or why they're destroying us systematically. In the early days we thought it was, I don't know... not America or Russia, they're both too fucked, but maybe the Koreans, the Chinese, with some crazy weapons tech, suddenly breaking cover and trying to take over the world with military might rather than cheap imports. We just did not know, because the minute they arrived all our tech shorted out. Mobile phones, radio, TV, internet, no signal anywhere. And all of a sudden every one of us was in the blind, transmitting without hearing, shouting just to get an echo. And while we were flailing around and hunkering down and heading for the hills, they destroyed everything.

You've seen those disaster movies. Godzilla, earthquake, tsunami or whatever other generic destructive force is being invoked. Mostly, the damage is to cities, especially New York, I suppose because of all the tall buildings the effects guys get to play with. A crashed skyscraper here, a crumbling Chrysler Building there, the odd flattened yellow-cab and the job's done. We infer so much chaos from the annihilation of so little: we don't even see the buildings still standing because we're too busy staring at the ones which have been wrecked.

We don't see the buildings still standing here, either, because there is nothing left standing. There are no tower blocks any more. No shops, houses, post-offices, supermarkets, hospitals, bowling-alleys, train stations, bus-stops, offices, cafés, theatres, cinemas, market stalls. There are no bars or pubs left, just flat-crushed smears of scorched rubble and ash. But there are no forests, either. No hills, no trees, everything crushed, slashed down, burned up. Flattened and blackened as though someone took a great burning club and just beat the shit out of the landscape. Which I suppose in a way they did.

Twenty-three of us left; no kids any more, thank God. I've got – I had – two girls. I keep forgetting they're gone. I wasn't at home when they came, that's why I'm here now. I don't know if that's good or bad, but that's how it is. The smell, even down here, it works its way in somehow, through the air-vents or the soil or something … it's like burnt toast. Night and day it tickles in my nostrils: I wake up with a start thinking something's on fire, and of course something is. The world, or the world we knew. I'm hoping we don't know everything, that there's someone else out there. A patch of land unburnt. People. Hope.

I'm not thinking about rescue. I don't even know what that would mean, now. But I really believe there must be someone, something, not a voice I'll ever hear because we're deaf down here – but maybe somebody, still listening.

So my eight minutes are up and Dan's going to wake any second now, I know that twitchy-nose thing he does. So here's the deal: I don't want you wasting your time trying to find us if we're all dead, so next week I'll record another message, put it out, add it to this one. That way you'll know we're still here, hanging on, and then depending on how fucked-up it looks out there, you can come and get us, or blip us somehow to say hello, or go on your merry way, it doesn't matter. Just so if you're out there and as lonely as we are in here, you can hear a human voice.

I haven't thought what'll happen if we don't make it, if I don't get to record another message, but I'll leave the transmitter on so I suppose this callout will just keep repeating. There you go, that's an easy sign for you: listen to the end of this message, and if there's one or two or more after it, we're still here, still alive. But if you hear the intro again and start experiencing severe *déjà vu*, well, I don't have to spell it out. Anyway, there it is. Good luck. We're thinking about you out there, down here. We'll hang on as long as we can. Cera Mulcahy out.

*

*

*

This is Cera Mulcahy, transmitting in the blind. Station 156, population twenty-three, duration seven months two weeks five days. We can't hear anything down here but we're reaching out to whoever can hear us, reaching out in the blind…

Bite
A.J. Akoto

Daylight consumed
and the frost clawed deep within it,

cold burning out colour:
black leaves, black bark.

Winter, lightless,
hours driven towards the longest night.

Then the watching hour,
waking in the deepness

for quiet battling with the self,
for gnawing out fear.

Or to feel the tipping point
where blackness quivers and draws

back, having come to its furthest reach
and found that day

has discovered teeth and turned
back to bite.

Daylight Saving Time
Lisa Kelly

In this house we are each in our own time zones,
living in a continuous present. I am locking
myself in my head, seeding furrows.
I am letting the chamomile tea cool, burying
the nagging thought, *the day is almost done.*

My son is recovering under a skinned duvet,
at least an hour behind my mean time
in a sub-tropical fug. He is lying on popcorn
seeds which failed to pop, red-eyed,
headachy from a sleepover with no sleep.

Above him, a demi-god in the attic, his father
is germinating an argument, his head
in files and next week. He is labouring
until the wee hours, measured in boy hours
as inconceivable light years ahead.

Grey Sky
Frank Rubino

Grey sky
silver like it never had the idea
of colour, colour not yet
invented. The walks are icy, rain freezes,
turns to slush.
We're safer on the street
where the cars churn and skid.
We want to stride but small
planted steps make our hips ache.

Out the train window, railroad ties
are bundled in a yard,
their top faces white with snow.

Why do I love them? Their straight edges
are not straight but jagged with crystalline facets.

On Reflection

Jill Sharp

When I look up
from my book I see
through the window the bare tree
the bare branches
shaking, rattling in the wind
on a grey sky
and I wonder what they are
like, these branches; what
is this moment
framed in the window,
and I mean to return
to consider the tree, but
when I look up
the window is dark –
there is only
myself, sitting
in a lit room.

Short Day: Solstice

Joan Leotta

As the solstice nears,
I pull out the candles.
I wake before the sun.
He tires easily, it seems,
in the season's chill.
So, I light candles,
festooning my house with
their brightness
against the dark outside.
Dancing in the flicker, I
fill my house with cookie smells
and songs of joy.
Light may be in short supply,
especially on that shortest day,
but what there is of it
will be for celebration.

The Blind Elephants of Io
Karen Bovenmyer

The silence is complete until
the rover's thrum breaks it–
this is no place to catch
sight of the elephants of Io – so
Rev takes us down one dune almost

weightless

and up another, fine silt waterfalling.
Io is the same size as Earth's moon
but pockmarked and yellow-red,
smoke-grey eruptions caused by huge
tidal forces from Jupiter's mass

like the ones pulling my heart
into the dust storm that would result
from telling Rev how I really feel
about that night we spent together
skin to skin – for survival – wanting

infinity

so close, but professional, me
wanting him, skin to skin, again
regulations be damned
and both of us as well
but wanting is not acting, not–

Rev kills the rover and my heartbeat
thuds loud in my suit. The windshield steams
with mingled breath. I see footprints in sulfur-dioxide
frost where the elephants walked last solstice.
They only come one day, the shortest day

a singular chance, a slow procession
one alien moving before the other
almost touching, the way magma flows
in a low gravity environment, like
a lineup of lava lamps in a sex den

floating

Rev grips my shoulder as the herd appears
over the next dune, all around us
tails flicking, trunks swinging just above the
clouds of moon sand, moving like nothing
else, the rolling gait of their namesake–

like but not the pachyderms of Earth. Eyeless
heads swing ivory tusks back and forth
while the plasma torus of Io's volcanic ejecta
glows behind them. Like a nimbus, their shapes
seem outlined in fire. The shortest day is ending.

I'm going to kiss him. I'm going to kiss
him before the elephants no one mentions
are no longer in the room. I'm going to
while he watches, his mouth relaxed,
eyes wide in wonder

Io is the driest known object
in the solar system, but right now
it is nothing compared to
my mouth

New Kinds of Weather
Karina Lutz

Muffled shocks
of thunder snow,
its lavender lightning
from high in the low clouds
muted and mistaken for
the arcing of transformers
where wind strains wires
from poles; but these
light the blizzard
from within
as chartreuse as new maple leaves and flowers
only paler.
Quickly all falls back to grey…
                         and grey deepens.
Indoors, lights flicker
as neighbourhood after neighbourhood
goes dark all over town,
one side of the street, then ours.
We light dusty candles and
remember how to trim
an oil-lamp wick, pile food from fridge
into coolers on the deck.
Overnight two feet of snow
thrown over them like a lumpy comforter
or moguls of the flatlands
and we are happy to be homebound.

Finally, as we shovel together,
a chance to talk with the Mormon neighbours
who declined the move-in pie.
That and solstice and the glee
of sledders make a short day
with an excuse to visit the widows
and the divorced.

That night a neighbour, still without heat, carries
his sleeping bag across the street
–no cars, still white–
miner's light on his forehead
beaming both ways.
A retired chemist, he explains to us hippies
why he hoped we might have
a hand grinder
for his coffee beans,
why they are so much better home-ground.

Watching Your Hair Grow Back in December
Marlee Cox

We must wait for the snow to
melt. Then, I can go outside
and sift through the soggy,
mottled remains of the last
year. When you shaved
your head, I snapped a picture
each day, watching the
new coat of black fuzz sprout up
and take root. I didn't ask
why you ditched your hair. Maybe it
was because someone ditched you,
and I really didn't want to bring that up.

In my yard, I found: skin cell
residue, thirty-eight cents,
an amethyst pin meant
for a wool coat at a funeral,
and a nametag: *Hello. My name is
Ice. I am a bleeding boy.*
These things remain. These – the
dress, white as movie-star teeth, and the
sad, smoky smile you gave me
for my birthday.

Our neighbours built a fence
of doors, each its own
shade of purple
or regret. I asked
my mother: *Doors let
people in.*

I asked you. *Doors keep people out.*

Star: Light
Pat Tompkins

Ablaze, drenching us with heat,
dictating what we do.
The cold dark of its absence.
Traveling great distance,
arcing across the sky.
Magically mundane,
clock and calendar.
Swallowed by a dragon;
sacrifices to ensure its return.
Mirrored by the moon
and circles of stone.
Monuments to our first god.

Wonderwork
Pat Tompkins

no need for inventions with such mysteries
the unknowns remain the how and why

a mound forms the natural shape
for sun and fertility

such size, such effort,
no easy tribute, this sparkling crown

materials matter: massive stones
stories in spirals and chevrons

tales familiar and foreign as birdsong
to ornament is to honour

a calendar in quartz
a temple we may partly understand

celebrating the dawn of a new year
the union of the luminous world

in diminuendo
Scott-Patrick Mitchell

day ends as quick as
it begins with coffee,
cigarettes, dancing
muscles unslept, get
dressed

so asleep inside my clothes
i miss buses, trip over kerbs
and holes, imagine smoke
opens portals to some other
world

at work i lag like the computer
network, glitch and quirk and
irk, send error messages to
myself just to get something to
read

lunch is a quick munch of
chewing the crunch, eating's
a doing, saliva on too dry
roll, dreaming I'm at a water
hole

catch bus home, sugar
crash into low fly zone
gnawing bone, stomach
unclenching low atomic
moan

tonight the moon is
full bloom bright, coos
me to sooth, strip, sleep
and in dreams give in
to day's
            shortness

Proserpine
Steph Thompson

How the hours unspooled since you have left the hidden hollow
that was me-you
Already you are unfolding, smoothing, become the world's:
Each smiling face a ticking marker of the hour
Could I preserve the air within the balloons,
Or press the flowers I hold within a book that would never close
The pain so sweet is dulling, dulling.
I would rewind, push you back within. It didn't happen if
nobody saw.

 But like the kisses, this day will wash away, into drains
of growing life.

You run out of the tunnel, Proserpine, turning winter into spring
You bulb of a thing, exploding large into life and unravelling
the hours
I put into your skin, into growing your heart and letting
you listen to mine.
My centre is twitching, collapsing in on itself, the recipe
complete
The oven swept clean, scent lingering of freshly baked
beginnings.

You cry and I hear your mirth, your future in you already
To carry around until it screams to be let out
The world exists for you, in more than shades of red and splits
Wide into pale light, brightening, darkening, to repeat forever
Or all the forever left to me, in you.

Too fast. Too fast you go, swift as the day. Too brief, the hours.
And I, running forever after you –
I cannot catch you.

When I Asked if it Could be Tomorrow
Laura Page

When I asked if it could be
tomorrow already, I meant can
it be you already, here for advent's
last lineup. You said
lean back. The earth's axis
tucks the light into
strobing corners, gently,
gently folds you back against her
contours premature, under her conifers–
the only green that is shushing
now.
When I asked if it could be tomorrow
already, I could feel you strobing
yes.

Shortest Day at the Beach
Tim Cremin

No gulls – just one crow
to start the Darkness Festival.
Poor thing – one bleak note
like a rock caught in its throat.

I guess that's as high
as the sun is going to get. We must be
further north than I thought.

This Place
Tim Cremin

I won't forget this place, our being part of it
in summer's dense abundance of cascading shade,
and this meagre light of winter.
Whichever one I'm in, I'm longing for the other,

wanting to have them both at once,
to hear each one and their harmony,
like two violins in resonant movement

around and through and inside each other,
whole again, like we were before

the blast shattered us to pieces.

First Light

Ness Owen

Blanket wrapped
he sits at the side
of my bed, it's far
passed midnight
and we haven't
slept, we listen to
classics on the radio
suck boiled sweets to
stop my dry throat
I'm too old for his
white horses to
send me to sleep
but I'm too young
to give up. You have
to find a way, he says,
to stop living in your
own head. The gap
in the curtains lets the
moonlight slip down
the wall till it tips over
the horizon and together
we wait for first light.

On Winter Days in Northern Norway
Megan E. Freeman

I trekked in the morning dark up the hill to the art school.
Wore reflectors on my coat. Took coffee breaks in the *cafena,*
near the fireplace at tables strewn with ashtrays and saucers.
Ate flatbread sandwiches with egg and dill and caviar. Knitting
needles clicked beneath raucous laughter and the smoke from
hand-rolled cigarettes.

I never saw a polar bear.

I did eat reindeer steaks served with boiled new potatoes.
Wore sealskin slippers across heated bathroom floors. Set the
clock each night hoping batteries wouldn't die and leave me
unalarmed in dark confusion of night or day, prompt or tardy.
Faith in Duracell replaced the absent sun.

I never saw a troll.

I did ice skate on a flooded frozen pitch under an arctic moon.
Certain stillness and specific cold unfurled ribbons of fuchsia
and emerald, swirling and snapping across the sky in rhythmic
gymnastics of jewel-toned light. I gawked at the animation of
colour and cold, a dynamism still photographs couldn't capture.

I never saw a Viking.

I did nap naked on the sunbed each week.

Dreamed of sunbathing on a California beach. Woke in the dark afternoon to redress in parka and scarves. Trekked home through the narrow tunnel under the railroad yard. The artificial artery spilled artificial light from either end onto the ore-dusted snowdrifts and delivered me into the frozen street near the darkened church.

I tucked into bed each night with the fickle promise that again the sun would still not rise tomorrow.

Winter Solstice, 2016
Mario Duarte

the longest night any day faces
drops soundlessly to the earth, like snow,
slamming the day flat on its back,

but the day jumps back on her feet,
pins the night, face down on his ice,
with a power even the Mayans

misunderstood – it is not the end,
only the beginning of more light.

The Turning of the Year
Alison Craig

The shortest day is the longest night
dark will soon give way to light
spring will soon be within sight
and the earth keeps on revolving

The sun is weak, it's rays are long
for warmth our bodies yearning
and winter reaps a heavy toll
let's keep the fire burning

The shortest day is the longest night
dark will soon give way to light
spring is almost within sight
and the world keeps on evolving.

Somewhere it's dark, somewhere it's light
some take to their beds, others take up flight
for the shortest day is the longest night
when the snow it starts a-falling

We can hunker down and call on friends
tell our stories to the winter's end
when the crocus can unfurl again
and the cuckoo comes a calling

The South is bathed in midnight sun
while here up North night's never done
the hours from dusk to dawn stretch long
so raise a glass let's sing a song

To the shortest day and the longest night
with a beer or two by candlelight
for the new year's birth is clear in sight
and the earth keeps on revolving

Light a Candle
Juliet Desailly

When the dark, dark night seems never-ending
and you doubt that the day will ever dawn,
when the cold and the damp seep into your bones
and you feel you will never be warm.
When the fear and the doubt come a-creeping
and you're sure there is no one else there
that there'll be no tomorrow, the sun won't return
and all of your fears are laid bare.

Light a candle for joy
light a candle for love.
Just a little spark
lighting up the dark
to promise a new day.
Light a candle for hope
light a candle for faith.
Just a little glow
just enough to show
the darkness will not stay

All round the world
let them shine out to show
that living is for caring
for every one of us
a special day
for giving and for sharing.

Light a candle for peace
light a candle for life.
Just a little light
shining in the night
for our celebration.
Light a candle for one
light a candle for all.
Just a little flame
but it means the same
in every nation.

Mock Posh and Tatters
Moira Quinn

As I was going to St Ives,
I met a man with seven eyes
upon a mask, he looked askance,
said, 'Why aren't you going to Penzance?'
I laughed at him and shook my head,
'Why did you ask me that?' I said.

His seven eyes began to roll,
'Because,' he said, 'tonight's Montol.'
'Montol?' I echoed, 'What is that?'
 He blinked his eyes, took off his hat.
'Mid-winter Solstice night,' he smiled
 'and that's the night Penzance goes wild.'

I looked at him all dressed in black;
a tattered cloak hung down his back.
He carried a fiddle in his hand.
'I'm in the Turkey Rhubarb Band,'
he told me and began to play
a tune to mark the shortest day.

I listened to him and in my head
I saw the truth of what he said
The lanterns glowed, the people danced
in masks and cloaks throughout Penzance.
And on the hill the brazier fire,
the serpent dance, the Cornish choir
sent crackling sparks into the night
whilst all around twirled with delight.

Montol's a time for olden ways,
the Lord of Misrule and Penglaze,
the Raven King, the River of Fire
all come together and conspire
to make the darkest night take flight
and celebrate mid-winter's night.

LONGEST NIGHT

At the *Hotel de la Lune*
Sarah James

[Beneath the neon]

I

The man in 512 is trying to sleep
but he can hear his ex's breath
in the air conditioning's webs.

A constant hum goose-pimples dreams,
prickles his sub-conscious.
He wakes to the clunk of closed doors.

[Sleep/wake/sleep]

II

Down the corridor, Anna's hand fidgets
with the beads at her neck, as she recites
the delay that saved her. *One, two, three…*

Round, whole – the smooth cream
of these almost pearls almost soothes –
each one a minute of grace.

One, two… the tap of plastic
against plastic distracts
from the massive spider at her feet,

the flames in her mind, the bubbling
heat, that black on her fingers…
four, five… She holds to the count,

the solidity of its beat. If she focuses
on the numbers' repeat, the threaded beads

won't melt into fire-blown faces.

[Count/countless/miscount]

III

Tom's head is bowed. He sighs,
then pushes his sales figures away
and pulls open the desk drawer.

His hand stumbles on empty space,
and the Gideon. A money spider drops
from the ceiling onto his spreadsheets:

tiny black blot on tiny black squiggles
that refuse to add up
to more than last month's disaster.

[Figure/configure/disfigured]

IV

Next door, another 'Mr and Mrs Jones'
shock dust from the vents.
Beetles scuttle in the dented woodwork.

[Shock/ShocK/FauxSHOCK]

V

Room 518 is vacant.
But some ghost
keeps setting a 3am alarm.

The door squeaks,
the towel rail won't heat
and the hairdryer's broken.

The bathroom tap
won't stop dripping.
A dead daddy longlegs

guards the plughole.

[Drip/drip/dropped]

VI

Alenka watches a spider prowl
the corridor, playing hide
and seek at the edge of the carpet.

The black trap of her foot
hovers over it, then she turns
to stack the new day's linen.

Tiredness shivers through her,
eyes heavy as moons
caught in red spider webs.

The colour of poppies
on her grandmother's grave.
Memories are paper knives

that slit through the softness
of each white sheet
folded as Babica taught her.

[Fold/smooth/unfold]

VII

Waking early in 513,
Tina strokes her son's face;
his body curved in sleep

like a snail peeled from its shell.
She imagines the doll's house
they left behind swings

empty on its hinges.
At the dining room table,
a black bug waits, fork ready.

In the plastic kitchen,
beer cans squashed
to metal knuckles.

[Hide/hate/hide]

VIII

On reception, Billy bins his crisp packet
and looks at his watch: still early enough
for one last quick run-through.

He picks a spot on the wall to act to:
'I have had a dream, past the wit of man…'
From his cubby-hole stage, he bows

to the air's standing ovation.
While he wipes his brow, a spider spins
new threads in the hotel's *Lune* shadows.

Spooning
Abigail Beckel

Are you awake? we ask the sleeping
bodies of those we love. An active wish
for less loneliness. *Are you awake?*
Are you awake? The push of my finger
into flesh, the dent it leaves. The slow
groan of waking. Every shadow has a seam,
sewn to the knife edge of light – it can never
escape the fact that it's made of darkness.
I zipper myself to your now restless warmth,
knee behind knee, my body curled around
your back, my nose to your neck.
I breathe in your long, quiet breaths.
I am sleeping in sneakers just in case
night becomes smoke or shatter or day.
I dream my exhaustion is permanent.

How We Know the Cold Is Coming, *or* October
Abigail Beckel

My husband is unravelling the mummy
that chases him, all moaning and death.
He could have torn the fabric from the head
first and killed it, or started at the feet
to slow it down, but he grabbed at the midriff
and now the mummy wears a crop-top
belly shirt over wasted flesh still stalking him.
I laugh a little when he tells me this part,
despite the panic flared in his eyes,
his futile unwrapping fresh in his fingers.
He almost never remembers his dreams.
My dreams collect in every slumber like sighs–
in my dream last night, I had a hundred dreams.
Winter came while we were at the beach,
a giant 'W' on the skyline, frost hardening
our bathing suits tight to summer skin.
The snow whirled wild and thick, sticking.
The sand, the snow, small particles pressing in–
sand, snow, sand, snow, foam, frozen, vertigo.
Nature's teeth held us above, below, ankle-deep
in intensity and icy surf. It was deafening,
the endless lapping of darkness at our feet.

Vigil
Abigail Beckel

I lie down in their bed, pull the covers around us,
over my grandmother's bare ankles, silk nightgown,
the weight of her sleep after three days awake.
The first night without him, and I cannot shut my eyes,
watching the light angle through the hurricane shutters
and down the wall to an open book on his nightstand,
a glass of water tepid and still. His white hairs
on the pillow mingle with mine. My every movement
stirs his scent, his skin cells shifting around me,
sticking to my legs and arms. I breathe him in,
press the sheets against my face, aware that my body
will force his fragrance away, stealing him from her bed.
The last bits of my grandfather cling to me and together
he and I wait out the night, listening for her every breath
the way she had half-listened in her sleep for years.
Finally stirring, she stretches toward his spot, and I turn
to face her, a cloud of him swirling, rising between us.

Dunking for a New Sun
Bob Beagrie

This earth's longest night
Roams the backstreets
Winds down country lanes
To where roads peter out

The wind teases tears from eyes
a child crying in the darkness

We move inside
Edge deeper into the cave
The candle lit corners,
Watching the flicker
Bring our pictures to life

We have brought in the wild forest
Poison berries, pine cones, stars

The gathering of a year's spent seconds,
Toss the die, roll the ball, shuffle cards,
Drink, eat, kindle the sparks
Between us

While we wait
For the orange to resurface
From the bucket's swilling waters

A Little Favour
Wendy Gill

'It's just a little favour,' Becky said. 'You'll earn money, be able to eat as much as you like, watch their huge TV, all you have to do is look after Mitch. Please Ann, please do it for me, otherwise I can't go with them to Florida. You know I'd do the same for you.'

You probably wouldn't, I thought. 'But, I'm not good with dogs, you know that,' I said.

'All Mitch does is sleep.'

'Remember those sausage dogs chasing after us?'

'We were six, babe.'

I hate it when she calls me babe.

'Seven, actually...'

'Even if they'd caught us, what's the worst a little mutt like that could do; nibble your ankles?' she said, half laughing.

'It scared me, I still have nightmares.'

'Mitch can hardly walk, let alone run,' she said. 'He's seriously old, thirteen – that's like ninety in human years, right? Think of it as looking after an old man in a wheelchair...'

That didn't appeal either.

'All you have to do is feed him, and push him out into the garden once in a while.'

'What about asking your new friend Katie? You've put me off a lot to see her, lately.'

'Katie? She couldn't do it. Anyway, you're my best friend, Ann, you know that; this is a great opportunity, I wouldn't want you to miss out.'

'Bit short notice – has someone let you down?'

'No... Please Ann; he's just an old basset hound. You know;

the Hush Puppies dog.'

'No. I don't know.'

'I'll send you a photo, when we get off the phone. He's cute, you'll love him. Reminds me a bit of that guy you dated for a while.'

'D'you mean Jed?'

'Yes, Jed; all ears, short legs, fat, cuddly, but a bit slow.'

'I still love him, Becky.'

'See, I told you. Why don't you come over to the house and have a cuddle with Mitch? You'll see how docile he is; it'll be money for nothing,' she said, as if it was already decided. 'You're in between jobs, *and* saving for a car, right? It's perfect.'

'I don't know, Becky…'

'The Millers would *love* to meet you. How about tonight, around seven? We can go out to that new wine bar for a drink afterwards. I'll pay.'

'Okay, tonight; but I'm not making any promises.'

The people carrier pulled out of the driveway around four-thirty in the afternoon a week later.

I waved goodbye to the Millers, their three children, and nanny, Becky. It was too dark to see if any of them waved back.

I'd been chosen to look after Becky, when she'd moved into the area at the beginning of primary school. I've often thought, even at that young age, I must have had a dependable look about me, because we were all new that day. The teacher was right though; fifteen years on, I was still taking my duty seriously.

Becky knew that too.

Mitch remained in his corner of the kitchen, one ear draped over the side of his basket. Mrs Miller had given me clear instructions about Mitch, including administering medication for dog diabetes; a condition they'd failed to mention when I'd visited. Becky had also glossed over the terms of my assignment. She'd been busy getting the children ready for the trip when Mrs

Miller handed me a list of household chores that Becky apparently undertook after taking the children to school, informed me I could only eat the food in the fridge, then had to buy my own, and that she'd pay me when they got back. Then she stood over me while I set an alarm on my iPhone for seven in the evening and seven in the morning, every day, to give Mitch his pills.

No lie-ins, then.

She'd shown me the small white tablets, and how to press one into some dog food and feed Mitch by hand. If he spat it out, she told me I was to put it back into his mouth, clasp one hand around his snout and massage his neck with the other, until I felt him swallow.

Money for nothing.

'So that's it, Mitch, just you and me for the next two and a half weeks,' I said, crouching at his level. 'You're going to be a good dog for Ann aren't you, and swallow your pills?'

The doorbell rang, Mitch didn't move from his bed.

'What've they forgotten?' I said, flinging the door open wide. A man pushed straight passed me, into the house, as if being chased by a madman.

'Where is she?' he was already looking in other rooms. 'Where is she?' he started up the stairs, two at a time.

Mitch growled, but didn't move.

'There's no one up there,' I shouted after him, without thinking. 'Who are you looking for?' I could hear him opening and closing doors, checking all the bedrooms.

'Becky, where is she?' he screamed, on his way back down.

'Becky? She's not here; and whoever you are, you should leave too,' I said, still holding the front door open.

'Where is she?' He seemed confused, not knowing whether to cry or to explode with anger. That's when I knew that I'd seen him before.

'I told her I'd do it, and I have; now tell me where she is. Please. *Please* tell me.' He grabbed my shoulders. It was that mole above his right eye; so unforgettable.

94

'What did you do?' I asked, wriggling free from his grasp, still trying to place him.

'I've done what she said she wanted.' He was biting his lips.

You too, I thought, studying his face. Then I got it.

'Don't you work in that posh drycleaners in the High Road?' He nodded. 'I own it.'

'I'm afraid you've missed Becky, she's already left for Miami, with the Millers.'

'God, I've been so stupid. What have I done?' He paced to the door and banged his head against it several times.

'It can't be *that* bad,' I said.

'I've just left my wife and little girl, Katie, for her; the week before Christmas. Tell me, what's not bad about that?' he said, almost in tears.

'Katie?' I repeated, piecing together a jigsaw in my head.

'Yes, that's how we met. I drop Katie at school, before I open the shop. She's friends with Esther Miller. Becky said I'd never leave them; told me I had until Christmas.' He collapsed onto the sofa and started to sob. I placed a hand on his shoulder, and squeezed.

'I'll get you a drink,' I said, sensing a long night ahead.

Steve, as he introduced himself, unpacked his Becky story, item by item: how it'd all started when she'd commented one morning that he didn't look happy.

'I'd been having a rough time at home,' he said. 'She started coming to the shop. She has a way about her. She's very convincing.'

'Tell me about it,' I said; rewinding her endlessly critical comments about Jed, and her final triumph: *Never mind, Ann. You can do sooo much better.* In that moment, I realized how she had manipulated me into giving up on Jed.

Steve and I chatted with ease; interrupted only by the iPhone reminder a few hours later.

'Just be true to yourself,' I said, as he left to go home.

Mitch was fast asleep. I removed one of the little white pills from the foil pack, pushed it into a lump of dogfood and held it under his nose. He groaned.

'Yum, yum?' I said. Mitch half opened one eye, but went straight back to sleep. I held the food to his mouth, still no response. 'Walkies, walkies!' I said, as if motivating a toddler. 'Meeeow, meeeow!' I thought that might get a reaction. *Nothing.* That was one truth Becky had told; all Mitch did was sleep.

I wouldn't like to admit the smell of dog food had got my appetite going, but I decided to temporarily abandon the mission, and check out the contents of the fridge. Not so bad; handmade meatballs in tomato sauce, various cheeses for after. I polished off the meatballs with a glass of sherry; the only bottle left out of the locked drinks cabinet. Then, like Christmas presents, I started to unwrap the cheeses; salivating as the aroma intensified. It was the happiest I'd been all day – until disturbed by a cold dampness at my ankle – Mitch was nudging me with his nose.

'Mitch! I'll get your pill.' I tried again with the lump of medicated dogfood, but he wouldn't open his mouth. Giving up, I returned to the cheeses. He nudged me again.

'D'you want some cheese, Mitch?' There was a soft goats' cheese I'd be able to push his pills into, I held a small piece out to him as a test. He devoured it.

Mission accomplished. After a celebratory glass of sherry, I headed upstairs for a bath. Mitch followed me to the bottom of the stairs.

'You're not allowed up here,' I said, looking into his doleful eyes. As soon as I was out of sight, he started to whine. Several times, I went halfway down the stairs to reassure him that he wasn't alone. He cried all the time I was soaking in the Jacuzzi bath. I put on warm clothes to take him for a walk, but he wouldn't move. I coaxed him into the back garden with cheese, and we stood together, gazing at the moon and stars, until he found a comfortable spot to do what he needed to do. Then I had another sherry and talked – to Mitch – unpicking the mess that was Becky, hoping Steve's wife would be forgiving.

Mitch was quiet when he was with me; otherwise he cried. I read to him, watched films with him, sang to him; trying to get to bed each time he settled down. I googled 'How to stop your dog whining', the consensus was to ignore him. My eyes were burning with tiredness; it was just after four. I hugged Mitch – he licked my face – I told him we both needed to sleep; I said goodnight and went to bed with my earphones in, playing music.

The light woke me. I sat up. A white earphone fell from my ear. Checking my phone, I saw the screen was blank – the battery had run out. I ran downstairs to see the time on the cooker; it was after eight. Mitch was lying peacefully in his bed.

'Sorry, Mitch, I'm going to have to wake you again to give you your pill,' I said, smiling in his direction. Kettle on, I reached for the pills and goats' cheese and approached his basket.

It was his complete stillness. I bent down in the hope I was wrong; that I would feel his breath on my face.

'Oh, Mitch,' I kissed his head, and cried.

Mrs Miller was quite nice, when I phoned her with the news; as though she'd been expecting it and was relieved it had happened when the children weren't at home. She asked me to take Mitch to a pet crematorium. The nearest was the other side of London. I rang a few cab companies, but they didn't want to know. I needed someone with a car, who was strong and understanding.

I rang Jed. *Be true to yourself*, I thought.

'I've been so stupid, Jed. Can you forgive me? Please? Can we start again? I can explain everything...'

'Ann! I thought I'd never hear from you again. I'd love to see you. Now I believe it's Christmas! Of course I'll help.'

Jed helped me say goodbye to Mitch. Then, we talked.

Back at the Millers', I wrote a note for Mrs Miller. Then I wrote one for Becky, requesting she do me a little favour and leave me alone from now on.

My duty was done.

Mouse
David Mathews

In a storybook she would have a name, Mina perhaps, to suit her cute tail and whiskers and the mob cap and apron that she would wear to sweep and dust her pretty mouse's house. But this is rough nature. Mouse has no cap or broom, and the start of a cold, stone hard December night in a Balkan thicket is not the time or place to be sentimental. She is just a mouse.

As a secretive animal she is disregarded by most of the world, but attractive to larger, wild things that need to eat. The dark suits her, but is perilous, full of eyes well made to detect her kind.

What are her chances?

**

The child entering the wood does have a name, Mineta.

What are *her* chances?

'Not far now,' says grandmother, holding her hand. 'Once we find a hidey-hole, my little mouse, we will be safe and you can sleep.'

**

In her nest of straw and hay mouse has been asleep, away from the snorting daytime creatures with their galumphing hooves.

These monsters are quiet now in their sties and byres and in the corners of fields, though all that matters to mouse is that they are no longer trampling the woodland fringe. The menace at night is elsewhere. Those eyes, they come with tooth and talon, claw and beak.

As the light disappears, mouse stirs, pokes her head out of the hole. Her first movements are staccato: a stretch of legs, a pause to check for footfall or the whoosh of flight, another stretch. *Listen, move, listen, move* – all at top speed, twitchy. Nose the air; *go, go, go!* A dash across open ground brings a big seed, and a root to protect her while she gnaws.

The seed is good. She will need many more tonight, though she has no sense of number, nor of the coming snow, or frozen ground, or the need to grow her babies; only the urge to bite, chew and swallow. She knows, in a vague way, a fungal smell, knows that a particular rotting tree promises sycamore seeds. *Where?* Somewhere near – her whole world is somewhere near. As her nose twitches to pick up the direction, she hears another's sniff – and a rustle, the snap of a twig, something unafraid to make a noise. Her heart beats faster, her tail lies flat, but her ears prick higher – *left, left, there.* The sniff is closer, the smell not good. She curls in defence.

**

For grandmother and child the rustles and snuffles of the wood are harder to read than the sounds of the fields and the roads. *Listen, move, listen.*

'Granny, Granny, what's that?'

A scream echoes through the wood, brief and final.

**

The death, a few feet from mouse, takes a moment. Our little rodent urinates as the owl takes the rat made careless by his eagerness for supper. With her refuge now broadcasting her scent, the mouse chances an escape. Owl is occupied, tearing juicy, warm flesh, though it is not just owl that mouse should guard against. Even so she runs, and her panic fades, replaced by the urgent search for more seeds, a nut, a berry.

She does not have words. No word for mushroom or acorn. No word for rat. No word for owl, though for sure, an instinct for the silhouette of wings against the moon or an indigo sky. Always the same owl, lording it over his acres from dusk till dawn.

**

A truck engine screams towards the wood, stops. Truck doors slam, men call out, automatic weapons are cocked. The sounds mean nothing to owl or mouse, but grandmother shakes, and Mineta sobs and wets herself.

**

The base of an oak tree reeks of pig, a camouflaging smell for a creature like mouse who grooms when she is not eating, sleeping or feeding her young. The sow has left half an acorn, worth a dozen seeds, though mouse has to nibble it where it is wedged beneath a stone. A wary feast.

It is altogether dark now. Smell and hearing are her strengths, concealed feeding spots and holes too small for bigger beasts with their awkward paws and muzzles, her protection. Climbing is her showiest trick, though it leaves her ripe for being plucked from a stem or stalk.

Two beechnuts occupy half an hour, an age for a busy creature, not that she keeps track of time. But she is watchful, leaving the second nut as the sound and smell of fox come downwind. Under the tree and up inside she goes. Heavy rains have washed the earth from between the beech's roots, but even so, fox's paw cannot turn the corner as far as mouse can scramble. She feels his panting as his nose pokes in, foul, hot. If she had imagination, she might hope he would get stuck and be set upon in the morning by a dog, but all she does is shake and piss.

Fox leaves. He does not lie in wait. Perhaps he judges mouse a poor mouthful – her pups are too tiny yet to have swollen her – or maybe his reputation for being crafty is over-played.

She waits, then scuttles, smells, extracts seeds from late sloes, stands erect, listens. She hears leaves being brushed past, twigs cracking, not distant, but going away. She runs to another abundant bush.

**

The truck engine starts, doors slam, the engine revs and fades towards the river.

**

A berry rolls into a hole, and mouse follows. Her footing gives. Not a loose twig, more supple than bark or a root, something alive – long, scaly, coiled.

Sssssssssnake.

Mouse freezes.

Snake does not move his zigzag back. His tongue does not flicker, he does not raise his head. Snake is waiting, cool, calm, slow. Waiting – oh, lucky for mouse – waiting for the spring, waiting to wake from his winter's sleep when the sun makes it worth his while. Right now mouse could tickle snake, tweak his nose, pull his substantial tail – if she had a mind to, if she had any mind to spare from feeding and staying alive through the night.

On the breeze comes the smell of the old rotting tree, the one that means the seed cache. Greedy, she runs, grabs one of the seeds, another, another. The hoard has been raided and half the seeds are gone, but no matter, seed by seed is what counts.

**

'Stay here, under these bushes, behind this tree,' grandmother says, 'they will push the wind away. Take care of Dolly, she might be frightened, because she's not a big girl like you.'

'The tree feels all rough,' says the child. 'It's horrid, like the men.'

'No! This is a nice tree. His bark is a bit wrinkled because he's old, like me.'

'Do you mind being old, Granny?'

'Not all the time. Sometimes it is better to be old and not noticed. But now listen, my best girl. Granny has to go to the village the other side of the river, very quietly, on tippy toes, to get food and news. I will find a friendly person – there is always one. You have this last bit of sausage and my shawl. The sausage will fill your tummy, and the shawl will keep you warm. I need you to do a special job, to look after our bundle. Can you do that? Like you did when Granny went to milk the goats? You can use it as a pillow; that will keep it safe.'

'Will there be creepy things?'

'Creepy things here go to sleep for the winter, like in our own country.'

'Like Mummy and Daddy? You said they went to sleep.'

'Yes, my little one, they did.'

'I'm thirsty, Granny.'

'Drink this. Slowly now… I'll bring back some more, and perhaps some milk.'

'Sing to me, Granny, before you go. I am ever so sleepy. Please. I walked and walked and walked ever such a long way. Sing me the song about the little fountain, like Mummy used to.'

'And then, sweet one, quiet as a mouse.'

**

As she fills her stomach and becomes less frantic, mouse senses an unfamiliar odour. Deep into the night, she has foraged well, but this new smell draws her, something extra to eat. Fat. Oh, oh, oh! – she smells fat.

She finds the fat with a new creature, breathing slow like the wind, lying among bushes, long, wide as a tree. The fat makes mouse bold. The creature has a loose, tangled covering, softer than straw or hay. Where is the fat? High. Mouse climbs, her claws snagging the twisted fibres. Like snake, the sleeping child does not feel her, and the body's gentle rise and fall does not trouble mouse. The fat is meat, close to mouth and nostrils, where air comes out in great gusts, stinking and hot like fox. But it is fat, it is fat, and mouse drags it under a woven layer, where she sets to work and does not hear a fluttering above her.

The owl sees the movement of the folds where mouse has dragged the nib of meat – an owl sees every movement – and he judges the range. But he cannot see precisely where to grasp his prey. An owl does not dive in order to scrabble around. Oh no, he strikes first time, or looks elsewhere. Or waits. An owl is patient.

Fox returns – mouse smells him and cringes – but fox is wary of mouse's unconscious protector, and keeps his distance.

The wood quietens, owl flies to a more fruitful hunting ground, mouse eats and, replete, rests unaware of the aerial threat and its passing.

In the deepest hour of the night something larger than fox rambles into the wood from the fields, heading for home. Not a hunter, altogether lacking stealth, but a busy forager, working hard to build body mass for the coldest part of winter and for her brood. Inquisitive too, placing a paw on mouse's sleeping host before lumbering onwards. The child stirs under the prying touch, whimpers, stirs again – and turns over, burying mouse within the shawl under a dead weight.

Mouse knows what it is to be squashed and clawed when the males mate with her, one after the other. She knows the discomfort of squeezing through a hole or a crack, her soft bones moulding to the shape. She knows momentary terror, as when the owl took the rat – but nothing like this. She scrabbles, but her claws are caught in strong fibres and the more she struggles, the greater her entanglement. She bites her ties, but nothing gives.

For minutes she strains and shits and wees and squeaks, but she is bound tighter and tighter. She continues to panic, but with no outward movement beyond such shivering as her bonds allow, it is her heart that is doing all the work, beating at a killing speed. A mouse's heart can do this for an hour at most, and it is three hours until a child would normally rouse itself.

**

Sharp cracks from across the fields wake the child, who sits up. Mouse is able to move again, though not easily for she is nearly spent. As her grim nest of the last hour falls to the ground, she fights one last time, and frees her paws. One leg drags, the muscles torn, but she makes it to the tree, and finds a hole.

The hole is deep, empty save for the remains of a nut and a few berries. She begins to forget, for she knows only the present, her memory unspecific for all but food.

Confusing sounds from large creatures come to her from the

world above, and she cowers. Earth falls in the hole, but no more than a mouse is used to, and she stays put, exhausted. By first light, when she emerges, she is strong enough to bite soft shreds from the discarded shawl that had imprisoned her. She carries them to her nest, and returns for more.

Doubting Thomas
David McVey

The roar of breaking surf gave way to a hollow swirling and bubbling as Sowerby's strength ebbed. He was engulfed by a cold, liquid blackness, darker even than the wild midnight above the waves. He exhaled salt water and gave himself up to the sea.

When he opened his eyes the darkness had changed; haloes of light were visible above the solid black of the sea wall. He was being held securely, and drawn back towards the land. Still only semi-conscious, he dimly felt himself being hauled onto a wet, slimy slipway that angled into the water. His rescuer placed him in the recovery position and coaxed seawater from his lungs; he gave a violent, retching cough, and passed out.

In the days after he regained consciousness he relished the warmth and light of the hospital ward, the vitality of the nursing staff, the firm, enveloping comfort of the bedclothes. The whole lexicon of human life, the rich texture of the land of the living seemed things to be craved. He determined never to let go of them.

A man and a woman sat by his bed. The man he knew, his publisher Ryan Savage. The woman, young, intelligent-looking, had simply been introduced as Sarah.

'I was trying to reconcile a couple of points for the lecture I was giving,' he was telling them. 'I didn't find the hotel room very conducive to thought, so I decided to go for a walk.'

'At midnight?' asked Savage.

'Yes,' he smiled, 'often do that. Whole chapters of *God's*

Obituary were written in my head during late-night walks. Anyway, I went down to the seafront. It was a wild night – high tide. No one else about. Just as I reached the sea wall, there was a huge gust of wind which knocked me over, and a colossal wave seemed to suck me under. I struggled but in that sea – I thought the lights were going out for good.'

'No word of your mysterious rescuer yet, by the way,' said Savage. 'Not a soul has come forward.'

'Perhaps we could offer a reward? It's such a fantastic chance; what a long shot that someone was out on such a night, saw me in the dark, and had the pluck and the ability to get me out. Someone really special.'

'A sort of angel,' offered Sarah.

Thomas Sowerby, the celebrity atheist, merely snorted.

Sarah left soon afterwards. 'Nice girl,' said Sowerby. 'Bright, too. What does she do?'

'She's a journalist,' said Savage. 'I thought we might ask her to put out some kind of appeal for your benefactor to come forward.'

'Good idea. Helpful publicity for the new book, if a little unorthodox.'

Next morning a nurse shouted to Sowerby that he was in the paper, and tossed a copy of the *County Daily Echo* onto his bed. He unfolded it and recognised his face on the front page. He began to read.

God's Obituary Author Saved by Angel?
by Sarah Michael
Mystery continues to surround the rescue of Thomas Sowerby, the militant atheist author saved from the sea at Donnethorpe during last Thursday night's gale. No-one has been identified as the rescuer, and since the incident occurred late at night in difficult conditions, speculation is mounting that a supernatural element was involved.

The Rev. Ronald Staithes has written a book on modern angelic manifestations, and he believes that Mr Sowerby may have encountered a heavenly messenger. 'This was a remarkable escape for Mr Sowerby,' said Rev. Staithes, 'and I think it quite likely that God has sent a rescuer as a sign to him to use his prodigious talents to more useful purpose. God has prepared some work for him, I'm sure.'

Every time the Ward Sister told Sowerby a newspaper reporter wanted to speak to him – and it happened several times that day – he barked, 'I've nothing to say!'

Weeks later he sat in Savage's London office. 'Amazing, isn't it,' Savage was saying. 'All that publicity: every tabloid, TV, radio, and still whoever rescued you hasn't come forward. There'll be lots of interest in the new book.'

Sowerby did not smile. 'What book? Who's going to credit a book written by an atheist when everyone thinks he owes his life to an angel?'

Savage was quiet for a while and then glanced up at Sowerby and asked, 'How are things actually going with the book?' Sowerby looked away. 'You did promise us that *God's Obituary* was the start of a trilogy. We expected at least the first draft of *Above Us Only Sky* by now.'

Sowerby took a deep breath, looked thoughtful for a moment, and then said, 'I can't concentrate on the book just now – not until this thing is resolved. Until I find my rescuer and get them photographed and quoted by the press, I'll always be the sceptic who was saved by the God he doesn't believe in.'

Savage said, slowly and deliberately, 'You're going to sit in a kind of writer's limbo until this rescuer turns up? Suppose whoever it was got tugged back underwater after they pulled you onto the slipway? Have you thought about *that*? Let me put the PR hounds onto it. They can produce a rescuer from central casting.'

'Great thinking, Savage. What if the real hero emerges –

worse, he sells his story to the press? Do you see the headlines? *Atheist Author Fakes Non-existence of God!* No, I've decided to book myself into a hotel in Donnethorpe and I've hired a couple of enquiry agents. I don't care how much it costs. We'll go door-to-door, we'll build up a picture of where everybody in the town was on that night if we have to. We'll find him!' Sowerby's voice rose sharply.

After the two men had parted, Savage phoned his superior. 'No, he didn't go for the publicity boys' idea. He's definitely cracking up. I've given him another month; if that doesn't do it we'll have to try to get hold of his notes and find a hack to ghost it.'

For two weeks Sowerby lived in the echoing winter wastes of a Donnethorpe hotel; he did not use his own name, and a new growth of beard and shaggier hair kept him out of the public eye in a town where he was now well-known. He grew well used to the wind-scoured streets and the narrow alleys between rows of houses that smelt strongly of frying chips. Everywhere there was the tang of sea air, and every night from his window Sowerby heard the surf which might have been the last sound he ever heard; some nights it was a distant whisper, but more often it was a rumbling, wind-churned roar that went on all night. Several times he shuddered suddenly awake as the surf-roar reached a crescendo, and the house shook.

As the investigation continued it became clear that most of Donnethorpe had been in bed by the hour of the rescue. Few hotels or boarding-houses were willing to open their registers for the night in question. In any case, following up the names would have been a huge task.

Sowerby switched his attention to the neighbouring village of Hutwistle which lay just a mile inland; it was just possible that someone from there had been driving along Donnethorpe promenade on the night. Perhaps they had seen what had happened – or, perhaps, had been the saviour themselves.

The main road ran just past the village, and a single minor road branched, gathered houses along itself, and became the main street of the village. As Sowerby walked along this street in the growing gloom of a mid-December evening, he felt a new mood of well-being and purpose and triumph: it was difficult to describe or explain this, but he had a real feeling that he was in the right place. This new stage of the investigation, he felt sure, would prove to be worthwhile and rewarding. There was something, a sense about this place.

The main street was quiet; the only other person Sowerby could see was a stout lady with a dog that was sniffing around the base of a lamp-post. It gave up its interest and the pair made to cross the street, moving out of the aura of light. Sowerby watched as a car screamed round the distant bend, accelerated, and bore down on the woman. She had reached the middle of the street but seemed transfixed with terror. The car started to brake. In only a few yards it would strike the woman. Sowerby saw that she could not move and he ran into the road, threw himself into the air and grabbed the woman with both arms. They landed with a dull thud just short of the pavement. Sowerby lifted his eyes to see the car screech to a stop some distance beyond where the woman had stood. The driver looked out, saw no movement from the two figures, and hurriedly drove off, tyres squealing.

Sowerby rose to his feet. The woman had bumped her head and was barely conscious, but there did not seem to be any serious damage: as her uninjured dog whimpered at her side, her hand lifted feebly to pet it. Sowerby, too, had sustained a blow to the head, and in his confusion could only think about returning to his hotel to rest.

Sowerby woke up next morning with a severe headache, and a vague sensation that the previous day had been an eventful one, yet he had no recollection of it.

Over breakfast he tried to recall the events of the preceding day: his body bore a galaxy of bruises, and his head throbbed. Had he been in some sort of trouble?

One of his investigators arrived. 'Would you believe It?' the man said, throwing a newspaper at Sowerby, 'If only we'd got there half an hour earlier we could've nipped this in the bud. Where were you, by the way?'

It was an article in a national tabloid. Sowerby read:

New 'Angel' rescue in Yorkshire
By Sarah Michael

Last night, in the sleepy Yorkshire village of Hutwistle, Mrs Gladys Arthur was wrenched from the path of a speeding car by a mysterious stranger. There is no doubt that the stranger saved her life, but he or she has not come forward. The incident happened just before 7pm in the main street of the village. 'I was out walking Sparky my dog,' said Mrs Arthur (52), 'when I crossed the main street. A car came out of nowhere and I felt myself being pushed out of its path.' Mrs Arthur bumped her head on the pavement and suffered concussion. The driver did not stop, and has yet to be traced. Police enquiries are continuing.

Mrs Arthur is a member of the local Methodist Church, and adds, 'God sent an angel to rescue me. I've no doubts about that.'

The incident occurred only a mile inland from the scene of the dramatic rescue of atheist writer Thomas Sowerby last month, also attributed to angelic intervention – though not by Mr Sowerby.

Sowerby finished his breakfast, went up to his room and packed. He carried his cases downstairs and settled up at reception.

As he waited on the station platform all curiosity about his lost evening evaporated. It didn't matter. Nothing did: certainly not the investigation. Angels were everywhere and he was doomed to be seen as the atheist that God had believed in. *God's Obituary* would remain a trilogy of one.

What He Doesn't Know
Frances Gapper

I've baked pies in the old bread oven and left a covered bowl of dough to prove in the boiler cupboard. My feet ache from being on them all morning, pattering back and forth – the kitchen is huge and the pantry off down a corridor. At least I get plenty of exercise. There's an old well in this kitchen, covered by the flagstones, at least so my mother-in-law once told me. *Crazy old bat*, the men laughed – but you can still see the flood line from 2005 on the wall by the door. Our farmhouse stands well above the river, so where did all that water come from? Off the moor, maybe – Peter thought so, and the field drains have since been improved.

We eat in front of the TV. I watch as he mashes the gravy from his pie with his potatoes, then forks it into his mouth, watching the screen. Where does he put it all? He's been wearing those jeans since the year we wed, 1992. His face is dark and hollow-cheeked, the opposite of my plump blondeness.

Stacking the plates, cutlery on top, I say 'Pudding. Don't stir, I'll bring them both in.'

I open the green panelled cupboard that houses the boiler, where earlier I cleared a space among the pillowcases and tea towels to set the dough in its pyrex bowl. Since then it's risen high, formed a muffin top. It needs knocking back. I put the bowl on the table, then lay into the dough with clenched fists. But it's strong and refuses to be diminished, to fall with an air-punched sigh. It pushes back, fights my hands, as though trying to leap from the bowl. I feel my face tighten in annoyance. 'Find your own shape, then,' I tell the bowl's contents. The kitchen is warm enough, womb enough, to foster and form. I dollop cream on apple crumble.

An hour later Peter yawns and stretches, ready to turn in for the night, but then it's the news and more importantly the weather, and he falls asleep in the high-backed chair that used to be his dad's. I slip out to the kitchen, whisper 'Are you ready?' For answer, two podgy arms encircle my waist, a sticky kiss lands on my mouth. 'Here now,' I reprove, 'I'm not him.' I unscrew a jar of currants and prod eyes into the girl's moon face. 'Wait for him in our bed,' I say. 'Embrace him and let him plunge between your buttery thighs. Be good food to him.' I slap dough girl on the buttocks and watch her scamper giggling upstairs.

At midnight in the star-speckled dark I cross the farmyard and hurry down the lane. Who'll be waiting by the bridge tonight? Here's Marilyn the goth, bare-armed and shivering; squarely built Gail; and of course Janet, in her waxed Parka from the barn shop that sells discounted outdoors gear. And the sheep, in the back of Janet's Land Rover.

'Right, let's get going,' Janet says. The Land Rover climbs a tree-shrouded lane, bumps along an unmade road. Tonight's moon isn't full nor a clear quarter, she's gibbous, vapid. Gail and Marilyn sit behind us, holding the ewe. Hooves scrape on ridged metal.

We stop at the usual place, by the angry river. The sheep's legs are bound, Janet clips wool from her neck, slashes her throat; she lifts heart and lungs from the body cavity, dumps the intestines in a bucket. The eviscerated beast is hoisted up to drain from a tree. We have plenty of blood for the offering. Janet asks me: 'Are you the volunteer?' I nod.

'Dart, Dart, cruel Dart, every year thou claim'st a heart.' The sheep's blood is poured on the fast-flowing water, swallowed by the darkness. I undress and plunge in after. The water's cold as death. I gasp twice, then immerse myself. *A willing sacrifice*, I say to the river in my mind, *take me*. She appreciates the gesture, but she rarely takes a woman, although every year that we don't do this, there's at least one death by drowning in the local paper, or a catastrophic flood. For now though, she's appeased. I get out and Janet wraps me in the towel that she always remembers to bring.

Beneath the ancient stars, on the bare moor, I feel alive.

This is it, I think, *where 'it' is.* Although I'm so cold my teeth rattle, I'm far from tired. I want to stay out here forever. While I dress, the others lug the carcass on to a plastic sheet in the back of Janet's vehicle. 'I'll drop the meat off tomorrow, at around eleven,' she says. 'Loin chops for you, Gail?'

Tomorrow the dough will be back in its bowl, quiet as a good wife. I'll make sweet bread rolls and he'll tear one apart, cram it in his mouth, maybe while totting up the weekly accounts. If I ask him a question he'll stare at me with dark encircled eyes. And I'll wonder, as I sometimes do, how much he knows.

Dancing to Silence
Neil Brosnan

It must have been the rain that woke her, she decides, listening to its stuttering staccato against the windowpane. She lies still for some moments before springing to a sitting position and flinging her pillow through the darkness of the bedroom. Sighing, she reaches for the other pillow – the one on which his scent still lingers – stuffs it beneath her head and, hugging it fiercely, cringes as each new squall-driven wave fractures and splatters against the glass. Though not yet dawn, a robin trills from the back garden.

She blinks at the green digital truth of her clock radio. She groans; her throat hurts. Rolling free of the duvet, her toes locate the faux fur softness of her slippers. Her fingers have already tied the belt of her dressing gown before the truth cannons into her breast: she is alone in the house – she has been ever since…

The blue-white glare from the florescent ceiling tube makes the kitchen feel even colder than usual. She flicks the switch of her electric kettle and as it begins to crackle to life she looks around absently for her cigarettes. But she doesn't have any cigarettes; she hasn't bought cigarettes for almost two months, not since she had become aware of his dislike of the smoke. In truth, she had been glad of the incentive to quit; thanks to him, this is her most successful attempt ever to kick the habit.

The kettle clicks its readiness. She spoons a generous measure of coffee into her favourite mug, inhaling the rich bouquet as the boiling water reacts with the grains. She stirs the mixture for a moment before opening the fridge, only to find she is out of milk. The thought of drinking coffee without an accompanying cigarette is bad enough, but without milk as well?

She battles though an array of empty wine bottles. Success: the vodka bottle is almost half-full. Her hand shakes as, watching the tiny brown bubbles explode, she adds a splash of the spirit to her mug. She stirs again before raising the mug between her palms and taking a cautious sip. Swallowing almost without tasting, she winces as the hot liquid blazes through her oesophagus; she adds a little more vodka – just enough to ease the sting – and then takes a decent mouthful.

The robin's song has competition now: the deeper, richer warble of a blackbird; the 'teacher-teacher' chirrup of a great tit; the dreamy cooing of a woodpigeon; the harsh rasps of a magpie. He would have been at the window by now. Unconsciously, she raises a bleary eye to the slashes of strengthening daylight that have forced their way through the heavy curtains. Sighing, she sways to her feet and kills the lights. She doesn't need to be reminded of the disarray of the kitchen, the clutter of mugs and glasses on the worktop or the scatter of unopened mail on the dining table. How many coffees has she had? She wonders, watching the dregs from the vodka bottle drip in dissolute silence into her steaming mug.

This is his fault: she'd never run out of milk when he'd been around, nor had she needed to seek solace in her drinks cabinet. Orla had warned her that no good would come of welcoming him into her home, that the whole charade was doomed to end in tears. Orla is never shy about telling others how to live their lives; Orla has all the answers. Yet, Orla is the one still living with her mother, Orla is the one who hasn't had a date since Ireland drew with Germany in the World Cup, and it's Orla who is still doing the job she'd taken for summer holiday pocket money when she was sixteen.

But he hadn't proven the liability that Orla had forecast, and he certainly hadn't been a drain on her time or her resources. He had demanded a degree of affection, yes, but she had given willingly and had felt rewarded in the double for every moment she had spent in his company. She can almost hear his breathing now; feel the comfort of his warm body and the rise and fall of his hirsute chest; the sensation of him nuzzling her neck; that thing he did with her toes. It had been a wonderful Christmas: night after night curled up together on the sitting room couch, watching old soppy TV movies before a blazing log fire.

Though of course, he hadn't been included in her invitation to Christmas dinner with her parents, he had behaved impeccably when they had come to lunch on the following Sunday. Clearly, there had been reservations on both sides, but he had seemed equally nonplussed at both Dad's aloofness and Mum's outright hostility. While the meal itself hadn't been without its tensions, Mum had admitted during the wash-up to being somewhat impressed by his general demeanour – this, while he had Dad cavorting like a ten-year-old through the snow in the back garden.

Mums are difficult to understand at the best of times: in the years when you'd most wanted to go out, they wouldn't let you; but just as soon as you tire of the rucking and scrummaging of the twilight jungle, they start ranting and raving about perms and poodles. Dads, on the other hand, could well be closet water bailiffs: they spend a lifetime telling you how there are many more fish in the sea – until you try to land one.

There is a dull thud on the window. Pulling her robe more tightly around her, she veers towards the back door, and then pauses. It can't be – it couldn't be, she reasons; she turns around and starts slowly up the stairs. She almost gags on entering the bedroom; when had the place become so stuffy? Squinting, she pulls back the curtains and, opening a portion of the window, takes a couple of deep breaths. The yard is a mess: the dead leaves; they'd had so much fun collecting them into little piles but they've somehow gravitated back to lie where they had originally fallen. The few items of clothing she'd hung on the line when she'd last done a wash are now lying shapeless, soiled and unrecognisable among a mishmash of take-away food wrappers, crisp packets and other debris. Turning around, she almost trips on the pillow she had earlier discarded; she bends to retrieve it and then discovers the milk carton. She has no idea how long it's been there, but it now seems as if an entire eco system is flourishing within its mysterious depths. Holding her nose, she gingerly lifts the offending container between thumb and forefinger and lets it drop to the yard below. She closes the window, draws the curtains and returns to bed.

She knows she should sleep, and she tries to, but the excess of caffeine has set her heart pumping, her pulse racing. She tosses and turns, fluffs her pillow, then flattens it, and then repeats the process with his pillow. She tries both pillows, then none. Nothing works, and the racket from the birds has become even worse. There are jackdaws now, squawking, squabbling, skittering – probably scrimmaging over the gunge from the expelled milk carton.

She should get dressed; she needs to go out – to a shop. She tries to visualise a list: milk, wine, maybe a pack of cigarettes. She is probably out of food as well – she is even out of vodka. She will have to shower first; she must look a proper sight; it's serious when she can smell herself. She shrugs out of her pyjamas.

The bathroom stinks; had she been sick? She shudders, her features contorting with each frightful stab of flashback. She flushes and then covers the toilet bowl. She swivels the showerhead to sluice the base and then squeezes copious splashes of disinfectant followed by a generous dollop of bubble bath. After bombarding every corner of the room with air-freshener, she finally engages the shower and embraces the soothing power of the cascading water.

Her head is clearing; days are separating from each other and from the nights that should have divided them. She wondered if Mags or Jenny had been trying to contact her. Perhaps not, she decides; hadn't all three of them hit the pub straight from work on Friday evening? They are probably just as hung-over as she is.

She had been with Mags and Jenny on the night she'd first seen Tom, when leaving the take-away beside their Insurance office. Though no verbal communication had taken place, she could feel herself being seduced by his amazing hazel-green eyes. At first, the girls had been dismissive of her decision, but once they had realised she was actually serious, their cynicism had quickly morphed to support. But it had been a mistake to convey her thoughts to Orla next day. Greatly underwhelmed, Orla had erupted into a tirade about alley cats, and had insisted that his type couldn't be changed. He was too set in his ways: he would never be content just to sit at home all night; when the night would call, he would answer. Yes, he could be the one who would finally break her heart. When she'd asked Orla if she actually knew Tom, she had to admit that, while she didn't actually know him specifically, she knew his type, she might even know him by sight.

He had been in exactly the same place at the same time a week later. Mags and Jenny had instantly made a bee-line for him, causing him to turn tail and disappear around the corner, but she had caught his eye for an instant and he had given that look again, as though seeing straight through to her very soul. The girls had exchanged knowing glances when she had declined their invitation to a coffee in their apartment. She gave them a dismissive wave as their front door eventually clicked shut. With ever-strengthening resolve she turned to retrace her steps back to the chipper. He was still there, less than a dozen paces away. He approached her with quiet, controlled purpose; each step measured as though to a tune only he could hear, as though he was about to sweep her into a dance – a tango perhaps, with that soulful, saturnine expression.

She gasps; suddenly, the water is freezing. Hugging her arms to her breasts, she just stands, stunned and shivering, for some seconds before finally deploying her right hand to shut off the water while her left probes the shower curtain. Shivering, she shuffles onto the cold tiles, towels herself dry and slips her robe back on.

A bloodcurdling wail sounds from the garden; as the caterwauling increases and multiplies, she hurries to the bedroom window. Necks craned, backs arched, tails askew, a pair of black cats cautiously circle each other by the boundary wall. She watches them for several moments, the grace of their ballet belying the savagery that choreographs it. She wonders if the owners of those cats are standing in freezing doorways or maintaining all night vigils at draughty windows.

She hunts for her mobile and, muttering something about cats only doing what cats are supposed to do, eventually locates it on the floor beneath the bedside locker. Recalling the tingle of his whiskers against her cheek, the thrill of taking him in her arms, the warmth of his body against her skin, her hips begin to sway as, dancing to silence, she selects the number. The battery is low but she gets through.

'Is that Ted? Ted, it's about Tom. I was wrong; I acted too hastily. I am so sorry. We deserve another chance; I promise I'll be more understanding, this time. I want to take him back, can I come round – this morning?' He is silent; the only sound is the thumping of her heart in her breast.

'I'm sorry,' he finally says, 'but Tom is no longer here: Tom has been vaccinated, microchipped, neutered and re-homed. Would you like to meet some of our other cats?'

The Midwinter Wife
Cherry Potts

What's lurking behind the row of sheds at the end of our gardens?

Our long narrow gardens are left over from the medieval half-life this town forgot in the aftermath of the war. That's what Martin-next-door says, and his dad is the county archivologist or something, so I suppose he knows. Martin-next-door's dad says we got bombed to buggery because we were on the flight path to somewhere more important, and German pilots got bored or scared, and dropped their bombs on us rather than wait, and the upshot and outcome is that the council used it as an excuse to tear down half the street and build a massive block of flats. A couple more neighbours sold off their gardens in the sixties and more houses appeared along a new road built in from the lane, so that all that's left of the medieval heart of town is the Wall, which no one can touch because it's an antiquity or something, and our house, Martin's house and the one on our other side; three ancient dark rickety narrow houses in a row, with long, long gardens that you can't shout down when you call the cat in because he won't hear, so you have to go out in the dark at least half way, because you don't know where the daft beast is hiding, and yell really loud, and possibly shake the biscuit tin too.

Tonight the cats – Martin-next-door's Joker, and our Muggsy, are crouched up there on our shed roof, with their fur on end, making weird frightening guttural wails, and peering down into the narrow strip of brambles by the Wall.

'Break it up lads,' I say, and the wailing rises in pitch. Maybe there's a stray caught down there. I edge between the shed and the fence, and peer round the back of the shed.

It isn't a stray, it's a girl – no a woman, scratched, and bruised, and angry – and she's completely naked.

'Martin, pass me your jacket.' Martin has over-protective parents; you'll never catch him out on a winter evening without a coat, even in the garden.

'Don't get it dirty,' he says as he hands it over the fence, 'and don't rip it.' I suppose he thinks I'm going to drop it over some wounded creature. Maybe I am, come to that. I hold it by the collar and edge it round the gap. It is snatched from my hand. I look away, illogical given I've seen all there is to see, but there is something indecent about struggling into clothes in a confined space.

Then there she is, head tilted defiantly, Martin's jacket pulled round her, but not buttoned. Her face is a web of scratches – all shallow, and barely bleeding, and her dark hair is matted to the left side of her head.

'You've been in the wars,' I say, startled into sounding like my gran.

'Warrs, yes.' She nods smartly. Martin, on the other side of the fence is open-mouthed.

'How did you get into Ned's garden?'

It's a fair question, but given the way she's staggering, it can wait. An adult might be an advantage just now, but Martin's parents would ask too many questions we can't answer and my dad is watching cricket highlights from some match played in India, so the chance of his looking up unless we walk between the sofa and the screen are small.

I offer the woman my arm, and she grabs and holds on like she's a shipwrecked sailor. A waft of her scent gusts over me, sweat and mud. It takes an age to walk up the garden; the cats spit at us, and follow in low slinking runs. As we reach the final set of steps before the kitchen terrace, Joker, with a final hiss, and a be-clawed swipe at a bare ankle, hurtles over the fence and in at his cat flap.

Martin appears at our kitchen door, having whipped round the front and through our house. You'll never catch Martin climbing a fence in case he snags his nice corduroy trousers. He doesn't actually have leather patches on his jacket elbows, but spiritually they exist.

The woman hesitates on the doorstep, and puts all her weight on my arm to get across the threshold. In the neon kitchen light, she looks even older than I thought; not Mum's age, not nearly, but – in her late twenties perhaps. The matting of her hair is caused by blood.

'W-would you like to wash?'

She looks at me blankly. I rub the side of my head. She raises her hand, touches her scalp cautiously.

'Wash, yes.'

I can't place her accent: she's small and dark, but it isn't the accent of any of the farm workers I hear on the bus every day.

Martin looks anxious; probably worried she's going to get blood on his precious coat. I take her, as quietly as I can, up the stairs and into the bathroom. She stands staring while I get a clean towel out. I put in the plug and run the water for her, like she wouldn't know how. She perches on the toilet, the coat swinging open. She plays with the chain, swinging it from side to side, like a cat with a toy.

'Right, I'll leave you to it.' This time I sound like my father. I suppose I'll eventually say something that sounds like a fifteen year old boy. Possibly that would be more embarrassing. I shut the door and hear the faint splash of feet in three inches of water. I jerk my head at Martin, and we head into my room. He sits on the bed while I pull out my oldest jeans and jumper. I know I'm going to lend her clothes, and I won't get them back. I pile the clothes against the bathroom door, and walk quietly away.

'Why are we doing this?' Martin asks.

What I want to say is 'why wouldn't we?' what I actually say is 'Got to?'

Martin nods slowly.

'That's what I feel too, got to – but why've we got to?' I shrug, and start looking at shoes.

'Ned,' he says anxiously. 'Why?'

I settle on slippers, an unappreciated gift from some aunt I never see. I can't shake the feeling of obligation.

'I should go home,' Martin says, an unfamiliar vein standing out in his forehead.

'Don't leave me alone with her,' I manage to whisper. He sobs. The door opens, and she stands there, jumper and jean-waistband barely meeting, her hair tied in a dripping knot. There are grey streaks in the wet hair, and crow's feet and frown lines plain on her face now it's clean enough to see. No scratches. Martin stands, and she stretches out on the bed.

'Hungry?' I pretend I'm asking Martin, but...

'Hongry, yes.'

Martin looks panicked as I shut the door on them. I take the stairs two at a time. Dad is in the kitchen, peering down the garden.

'What's with that stupid cat?' he asks. I glance out. I can just see Muggsy pacing up and down. I open the door to call him, and hear him spitting still. Seeing that daft old tabby so upset frightens me, more than having a stranger who wants something in the house. Muggsy stares up at the light from my window and wails. I shut the door sharply.

'Rabies, possibly?' I suggest. Dad laughs and goes back to the cricket. I put together a plate of things I hope Mum won't miss – a piece off the pork pie Dad made last week, two tomatoes, a slice of bread, one chocolate biscuit.

I boil the kettle, and make a mug of instant soup, and a mug of tea. I put a slug of whisky in the tea.

I can't get the bedroom door open without putting everything down.

Martin is backed into a corner and bright red in the face.

'I'm going.' He says.

'Don't…'

'Leave you on your own with her? You left me.'

He yanks his coat off the end of the bed and storms past me. I look down at her, the jumper has ridden up, exposing an expanse of stomach and lower ribs, and the fly of the jeans is wide open. I avert my eyes from a glimpse of hair. I kick the door shut and hold out the plate. She swivels to sit up, and takes it from me.

She takes a bite from each of my offerings, passing them to me to do likewise. It has a feel of ritual, and I eat reluctantly, grateful for a large swig of tea-and-whisky to force down the normally treasured pastry on Dad's pie.

The tomato bursts under my teeth and she laughs and leans to lick the juice off my chin. I shudder under the aliveness of it, squirming away. I get a waft of her scent again, something bitter and spicy that I can't name. She downs the rest of the tea.

'Good?' I say shakily.

'Gud, yes.'

I take the plate and mugs down stairs, and find Mum draped over Dad on the sofa. She's early. Normally I would roll my eyes, but tonight I'm just grateful they are there. I dump the crockery in the sink and loll against the door jamb. Mum raises her head and spots me.

'Fancy a pizza?' she asks.

I nod. 'I'll go shall I?' Dad reaches for the phone. I slow-motion through getting the money from Mum's purse; methodically finding boots, coat, hat and gloves.

'Do you need the huskies?' Dad asks, observing my preparations.

'No,' I say. 'They'd just slow me down and argue over whether there should be extra pepperoni.'

'OK. Don't speak to any walruses.'

I don't hurry; the pizza shop is just on the corner, Giovanni won't have the pizzas ready for another few minutes. I breathe frosty air, and look up at the matt black sky, and stars that seem

124

unusually bright. Instinctively I glance up the high road, towards London, and am reassured by the sullen red glow beyond the half-hearted string of lights that signify the approach of Christmas.

I swing in through the door of Giovanni's. Marco, who is at school with me, is just boxing up our dinner. I hand my money to Giovanni and try to engage Marco in conversation.

'Busy, innit,' is all he will say. He pushes the stacked boxes across the counter. The three minute walk home feels like a blink, and I wish it would last forever.

We eat slowly, to the accompaniment of an incomprehensible thriller on TV. I'm almost asleep when mum prods me.

'Bed,' she says. 'I'll come and tuck you in later.'

'You will not, I'm not having you inspect my paramour.'

She raises an eyebrow.

'No son of mine is ever going to be too old for a goodnight kiss,' she warns. I scramble up and kiss the top of her head, and for good measure, Dad's bald patch.

'Don't milk it,' I say sternly. 'Soppy moments are strictly on ration.'

I go upstairs, dread filling my mouth. I try to wash it out with toothpaste and extra brushing. The bedroom is dark, and for a happy moment, I imagine she has gone. But her smell pervades the room.

I put the light on. She has bundled the duvet up around her, but there is no disguising the change. Her face is creased and lined and her hair is white as bone, and worse, her belly is swollen like a malnourished child, or …a pregnant woman.

'No,' I say, awed.

'Yes,' she says, between gritted teeth.

'Now?' I ask horrified, turning to call my mother.

'Now, yes,' she says, and her hand shoots out to grab me.

I turn out the light, and sit on the floor beside her as she gasps her way through it, her unbreakable grip cutting off circulation to my hand. I hear Mum come up, she stands outside my room for several seconds, before Dad calls something from the living room and she wanders to the top of the stairs, and forgets to come back. I hear them in their bedroom, and then their light goes out and they snuffle into silence.

She is groaning rhythmically now. I can't believe my parents haven't heard. She gives a long shrill gasp, and then sobs and the grip on my wrist relaxes. I can hear the clock on the old church at the far end of the lane strike. A second later, the new church, up the high road, joins in: a discordant jangle of midnights. She fumbles for a moment and then a soft gurgle joins her sobs. Cradled in her arms is a child. The smallest, most perfect creature I ever saw.

She looks up at me, and holds out the child. She barely fills my two hands.

'Take.' I stare. Is she giving me the child? 'Take,' she says again. She pinches the cord hard and it parts, neatly sealed. She closes her eyes, waving her hand vaguely at the window that overlooks the garden.

'Wall.'

I wrap the child in a t-shirt and tiptoe past the parents' room and down the stairs, unlock the back door, grab Dad's gardening jacket and tuck the child in against my chest. Muggsy rushes me, wailing and carrying on. At the first set of steps Joker joins us. By the time I reach the sheds, there are more than a dozen cats, most of whom I don't recognise. A particularly mean looking tom stumbles into my leg several times before I realise he's trying to guide me. The cats are ranged along the shed roofs and the Wall.

Muggsy leaps onto my shoulder, and grumbles in my ear. He steps down into the crook of my arm, so that he is right next to the child. I try to shield her and he bites my thumb. As I jerk my hand away, he stretches his head and sinks his teeth into the knot holding the t-shirt together, and picks the child up. Before I can do more than gasp, he leaps out of my arms to the shed roof, and in three strides is on the Wall. The child is almost the same size as him, and Muggsy struggles with his burden.

Horrified, I climb after him, the cats swarming around me. I hook a leg over and straddle the wall. Muggsy turns his head, and drops the child. I lunge to catch, too far away, too slow.

A man raises his hands and catches her. Where did he come from? Where did all these people come from? Beyond the wall, standing in groups of three or four, are twenty, fifty …hundreds of people. Muggsy hisses and leaps back into the garden. I follow his movement, and realise that all the cats are going. I turn back to look back over the wall.

There is no one there, just brambles and sycamores. I shiver. I scramble down from the wall – it is not as easy as getting up. I walk up the garden, with Muggsy keeping pace, his tail raised in cheerful anticipation of food.

At the door to my bedroom I stop to listen. I can hear Dad's uneven snoring from the room opposite, but I can hear nothing from my room. I push open the door. She has gone. I shake out the duvet, as though she might be hiding in it.

A single bramble leaf falls out. I pick it up and press it to my lips. It gives off a faint scent, bitter and spicy.

Life Between Lives
Sarah Evans

The pain eases, allowing Imogen to breathe again. Anger floods in to fill the lull. *I never even wanted bloody kids.* Yet here she is – *again* – standing at the foot of her hospital bed, knuckles white where they clasp the metal frame, a long night stretching out before her. No sign of Max.

She'll ring, turn the screws on his guilt. Hardly a fair exchange. She pictures him still at his client's offices, mind occupied with technical details. 'I'll get the first train back,' he'd promised. This from the man who'd kept on promising *this'll be the last before the baby,* then always needed just one more trip to Brussels.

Voice-mail. He can't even be bothered to pick up.

'Where the fuck are you?' She wants him to feel bad. Isn't sure she wants him to be here, not exactly. Can picture the overly patient way he will talk her through breathing exercises, as if lung function could possibly ameliorate this frenzied agony. He will remain endlessly sympathetic as she hurls obscenities at him, but not for one second will he understand. Not just the force of pain, but the force with which she does not want this baby. *This is all your frigging fault.* Not just the obvious sense – easy pleasure on his part – but he was the one who wanted family.

I'd do it myself if I could.

Ha! Easy to assert. Not like she could actually call him on it.

Fury builds. But pain is building too and obliterating everything else and it is all she can do to count the seconds before the pain once again slackens.

A lifetime later – fifty-five seconds on her mobile app – the contraction passes. It is disconcerting how pain can be so all-encompassing one moment and gone the next. Not entirely gone. Her back aches, her bladder too. But the scale is manageable for now.

She breathes slowly, the scent of disinfectant, of sweat, the tea-like smell of amniotic fluid. Hospital sounds filter through the walls, the rattle of trolleys and buzz of voices, but she feels utterly deserted. The midwife was here twenty minutes ago. 'About two centimetres.' She delivered her devastating news with a downwards smile. 'Bit early for pain-relief. I'll pop back soon.' Midwives are forever popping or asking you to. *Just pop along. Just pop up onto the bed. Pop your legs open.* They fail to understand the definition of the word *soon*.

She feels a fool, undergoing this a third time. She can hardly claim naivety. Somehow she forgot, not the fact of pain, but what it actually feels like – just as she lost sight of her earlier certainties.

All through teenage years, adults smiled indulgently and told her she was too young to know her mind, and was bound to change. She hasn't changed, not at all. She simply fell in love with the wrong man, a man whose opinions turned out to be fundamentally different to her own.

On early dates, they talked idealism, favourite films and much-loved music. She could never have fallen in love with a Tory, with a religious nut, with anyone sexist, racist or homophobic. Why had Max's ambiguity on the question of kids – *maybe, sometime, I don't really know* – rated less highly, when it was the one issue that allowed no compromise?

How had he not picked up on *her* views?

I'll leave him.

The thought is spiked and clear.

Fine, you wanted it, have it! She will pass the thing over, still covered in its birth gunge; she will get up and walk away. She can picture it so clearly, his look of shock and horror, except now the images are blurring, because pain is swarming in again, ratcheting up.

And up and up and up...

The band searing her body eases. She can breathe again. She is supposed to breathe during contractions, has practised her rhythmic grunting along with all the other mums-to-be plus partners at the ante-natal class. Max had joined in a little over enthusiastically.

I never wanted this.

Max is not here to listen. Even if he had been...

Her heart clenches as she thinks of her two daughters, aged seven and five, their silk-smooth skin, their intense preoccupations, their passionate engagement with life and their vulnerability. Never having wanted kids does not imply she doesn't love the ones she has. Obviously not.

She had not known that love could be so compulsive. That she would wake sweat-drenched and shaking from dreams in which her girls have died and be compelled to get up and tip-toe through the dark and look in on them and check their breathing…

Tonight they are long tucked up tight, staying over with a friend.

The moon shines outside her small window. Her own reflection joins it in the darkened glass, eyes round and startled. She jumps, realises that the jangle of noise is from her phone.

One new message.

On my way. Love you loads. Hang in there. Max xxxxx

Does he really think his crappy message will bring comfort? He doesn't even have the balls to ring her. She'll ring him. She'll let him know that the minute the baby is out it is his and she will be off. She will become herself again, that independent woman who operates so efficiently in the adult world of careers and getting ahead.

Except now the agony is starting up, the pain in her back that will ripple its way forward with the same unstoppability of an incoming tide.

The assault builds and builds. Everything is happening too quickly. She can't do this. She is failing to breathe – to cope. She isn't riding the waves, the way she is supposed to; they are dragging her under and down. Max could've chased after the midwife and a shot of opioid, if only he'd bothered to be here. She presses the red button, but it is hopeless. By the time anyone responds it will be too late; she'll already have endured the unendurable.

No choice but to cling on. To count the seconds. To grip the rail. To chant *fuck, fuck, fuck*, which is precisely the thing that got her into this.

Seconds stretch to days. The chant changes: *stupid, stupid, stupid.*

She knowingly offered herself up to this torture. And she would do anything, if only someone would make this stop.

The easing comes, but the certain knowledge of imminent pain leaves her hollowed out. *Where the hell has that midwife got to?*

And then – unlike Max – Lynda is here, *popping up*, a Mary-Poppins smile on her face. 'Everything alright, my love?'

I'm not your love, Imogen wants to say, *everything is not alright.*

There is more popping. *Up onto the bed. Legs wide.*

'You are coming along quickly aren't you?' As if Imogen doesn't know that. 'Your birthing partner still not made it?' As if that isn't obvious.

'I'll just go and track down the pain-management specialist,' Lynda says, 'and see about moving you to a labour room.' She pops off again.

Leaving Imogen quite alone.

She tries to remember her previous life. The one she abandoned because childcare is expensive and strangers not to be relied upon with a precious child. Max just happened to earn more than her, he wasn't slow to point that out.

Another wave starts, contractions beginning to merge one

into another. No sign of Ms Pain-Management.

Pain sharpens her thoughts to diamond needle points and she feels herself occupying a fleeting state of bardo, where she can know her former selves and recognise the future.

Her child is being born; she is being reborn too.

Very soon, she will become that new-made entity: the mother of a babe-in-arms, a woman whose needs, wants and thoughts are subsumed by the dictates of the tiny being she has given life to.

Soon she will be swept away under the tsunami of hormones. By morning, these thoughts will be hazy, disconnected, lost. She will be metamorphosed into a doting mother.

I'm Imogen, she thinks, *a woman in my own right. I never wanted kids.*

Left of Earth, Right of Venus
Pauline Walker

'Are you ready Daphne?'

A raspy, urgent voice says it three times before my tongue prises open oyster-shell lips.

'Daphne?'

My breathy *yes* fogs the visor of my helmet. The helmet is temperature-controlled; in a nanosecond the visor is clear.

My calves begin to twitch. I try to recall yesterday's hurried training in the simulator.

The body will experience involuntary limb movements due to the short amount of time that you will have had to acclimatise to space. This is normal, do not panic.

'Are you ready Daphne?'

No, but I whisper 'yes'.

'Initiating countdown. TEN…NINE…EIGHT…'

I wiggle toes and stretch my feet as much as I can in the suit to alleviate the tension in my legs. I'm sure Lucy was in control of her body seconds before the mothership delivered her into space.

*

'I seized the day Mum,' she shouted, hugging me and her dad after landing her first solo parachute jump. My heart had left its usual place and squeezed itself into my throat as I watched her fall out of the sky.

'O.M.G. Mum it's so amazing up there and at one point I didn't think I was going to be able to do it and…' the adrenaline made her gabble on, '…but I just went for it didn't give myself time to think and my cheeks…' she grabbed mine, pinching and stretching them like I needed a facelift, then she pounced on

Victor and blew in his ears '…and the wind, everywhere Dad, up your nose as well and I was diving head first for a long time what a rush It's amazing.' She clung to us, spent.

*

'SEVEN…SIX…FIVE…'

Why couldn't she be normal like other people's children? Ride a bike around the park instead of hurtling around BMX tracks? Swim a hundred lengths in the pool instead of smearing herself in grease to conquer the channel? Finish her training as a sports physiotherapist instead of disappearing from the face of the earth?

'FOUR…THREE…TWO…'

I play Chopin, trying to work out which fingertip controls the visor display. Right index finger. The visor darkens to red and a white digital countdown clock appears: seven days, six hours and forty five minutes to reach her and get us both back.

'ONE.'

The hatch beneath my feet slides open. I brace myself in the suit as I'm gently sucked into an airless vacuum. I forget to tread water slowly, to let myself get used to the permanent sensation of nothing beneath me, around me, and I'm flailing, a newborn chick, flapping my arms in the void. Breath batters teeth, I cough, splutter, throat spasms, no breath, wide eyes forced shut.

'Don't fight it, Daphne. Relax, we've got you. Remember how it felt in the simulator.'

I let go of everything I know and don't know and become a floppy ragdoll.

My helmet floods with pure oxygen.

'Breathe Daphne, breathe.'

Panting.

Longer breaths.

I open one eye to read the countdown clock: seven days, six hours and forty minutes. I switch it on, off, on, off, on, off. My visor dissipates, diffused red light darkens to black. Outside it's…

…pitch black…

…a pitch black panorama.

I hear Lucy's voice in my head and I repeat, 'Oh my God.'

'Daphne? Daphne? Everything okay?'

'Oh my God.'

'Don't worry Daphne. Everyone has the same reaction. Remember your training. We acknowledge how overwhelmed you're feeling, but you are not alone out there. We're all in space together. We are connected to you and you are connected to us. Okay?'

'Okay.'

'Good. I can't give you precise co-ordinates but you are somewhere left of Earth and right of Venus.'

I laugh with him: giddy, manic, hyena giggles.

'That's good Daphne, means your acclimatising well. Laughing in space is good. Remember to keep focused, use your memories when you feel yourself getting stressed, the times in your life that made you smile, made you laugh. This will be an easy mission if you remember the good times. Now you are descending at a rate of twenty thousand metres per hour. Look around you Daphne. Do you see the others?'

I turn my head right, left, strain my neck upwards; tuck in my chin to look down. There are hundreds of space suits dangling from umbilical cords connected to the undercarriage of the huge spaceship. I'm like them, a guinea pig providing valuable data.

'We're bringing everyone up in order to channel all the residual power to you to increase your rate of descent. The countdown clock will adjust automatically. Once you reach Lucy you must start ascending before the solar flares eruption hits in four days' time at eighteen hundred hours. Do you understand?'

'Yes.'

'We will get you there as fast as we can but it is critical that you persuade Lucy to turn off her manual override so that we can bring you both home safely to the mothership.'

*

'Looshy in de shky with diamondsh…' She pirouettes as she sings her favourite song. She makes us dance with her. I laugh at Victor who can't stay on his tippee toes.

*

Something hits my right foot and jolts me back and upwards.

*

I've swapped places with Lucy on the swing and she's pushing me so high I gasp as two collared doves whiz past my face, cooing before they land on top of an oak tree.

*

The arm of a space suit bumps and bounces off my shin and thigh. I grab at the elbow but I'm not used to the clunky gloves and can't latch on. I twist my body, forcing it to swivel. Our visors meet and I stare into vivid green eyes. It's not Lucy. The eyes smile at me and in a few seconds they are gone, to be reabsorbed into the mothership cocoon.

'Someone knocked into me,' I blurt out, giggling. 'I didn't see or hear them coming.'

'There's no sound in space, Daphne. Remember?'

'I want to hear it.' I realise how stupid it sounds the moment it comes out of my mouth. They're going to think I'm going loopy, I can't stop giggling.

'Left hand, little finger. Press it twice Daphne.'

Silence.

Unadulterated.

The urge to laugh dissolves.

I think I know why Lucy is here. Tears splash my visor.

'Daphne, our sensors detect a temperature spike. Are you okay?'

I'm trembling.

'It's the shock of the unfamiliar Daphne. Your mind is trying to process something you've never experienced before. Think of happy times Daphne and try to normalise your breathing. Focus. In…and…out…in…out…'

My heart reverberates through my skin, vest, suit. It finds

a way outside and pulses, heat-haze throbbing distorts the blackness. It won't stop, it happens wherever I look, here, over there, everywhere is pulsating.

'Your blood pressure's rising too rapidly Daphne. We're going to help you relax.'

Someone's screaming outside, I can hear them.

*

Victor lifts my veil and whispers 'I'm the luckiest man in the world.' And a year later when the midwife hands him a fish and chip wrapped Lucy, with her bald head peeking out from the blanket, his tears drip on my cheek as he kisses me and blubs about his two beautiful girls.

*

A series of images. Victor and Lucy, five; sitting on Victor's lap, Lucy holding up her crayoned picture of the solar system. An arrow pointing down from Earth, a house, door in the middle, two windows either side, match-stick Lowry mummy, daddy, Lucy.

*

Victor and Lucy, six; in the back garden one November evening, Lucy looking through the telescope, Victor crouched beside her squinting up at the sky.

*

Victor and Lucy, seven; day trip to the Royal Observatory in Greenwich. Afterwards, outside, squeezing Victor's hand, the excitement at what she'd seen etched on her face.

*

Two months ago: I'm crying, I've succumbed to one of those long weeping sessions when I'm curled up in the foetal position under the duvet and I'm howling and using acres of pulped wood forest to collect the eruptions of mucus from my nose because the love of my life is gone, malignant, aggressive, stage four, no hope.

*

'Mum, wake up mum.'

Lucy's holding my helmet steady. I sniff away tears and gaze into the most knowing eyes in the universe. It's hard to hug wearing a space suit but we try. My visors mists over as I chant her name and blow kisses.

'I knew you'd come.'

'You did?'

'You wouldn't leave your daughter to explore the solar system by herself would you?'

'Daphne? Daphne?"

'You don't have to speak to them at all, ever again, if you don't want to.'

'Lucy.'

'It's so peaceful out here. Can't you feel it?'

'Lucy. Why here?'

'I needed time to think.'

I press the countdown button and the digital clock appears: two days, five hours, seventeen minutes.

'A solar flare storm is coming and we have to get back before…'

'I can't leave.'

I'm impatient, '…the flares will destroy everything in their way.'

'I'm glad you're here, so we can say goodbye. I didn't have that with dad did I?'

I can't suppress the panic. 'You are my daughter and you will do as you are told.'

Lucy arches her eyebrows, spreads her arms wide to take in the universe. 'Really mum?'

'You've made us headline news all over Earth, the internet is going crazy: *Fifty-year old mother blasted into space to rescue grief-stricken daughter.*'

I push her away as she tries to link arms with me.

I look up. The ship… the ship. I squint, trying to pinpoint the grey vessel bursting with people, alive with adventure and expectation in the darkness.

What would Victor do if he were here?

The countdown clock says two days, five hours, sixteen minutes when Lucy floats back to me. I let her wrap an arm around my waist, lean her helmet-head on my shoulder. Panic and mania subside but my grief is heightened now we understand each other.

It's a week since I was plunged into the black panorama, with the countdown clock running backwards then forwards then slowing, until I no longer know the meaning of time. The darkness is changing; shot through with sparks of gold.

I swing away from Lucy and press the communication button. When I return a minute later, I nod and say, 'We both need more time to think.'

We hold each other…

…and drift in space…

…for however long it takes…

ABOUT THE AUTHORS

With so many authors involved, including biographical notes here would tip the book into another section of sixteen pages. You can find details of *all* our authors and poets on our website: www.arachnepress.com.

ABOUT ARACHNE PRESS

Arachne Press is a micro publisher of (award-winning!) short story and poetry anthologies and collections, novels including a Carnegie Medal nominated young adult novel, and a photographic portrait collection. We are very grateful to Arts Council England for financial support for this book and three others, a tour round the UK and our live events.

We are expanding our range all the time, but the short form is our first love. We keep fiction and poetry live, through readings, festivals, our regular event *The Story Sessions*, workshops, exhibitions and all things to do with writing.

Follow us on Twitter:
@ArachnePress
@SolShorts

Like us on Facebook:
ArachnePress
SolsticeShorts2014
TheStorySessions

MORE FROM ARACHNE PRESS
www.arachnepress.com

BOOKS

COMING SOON:
With Paper for Feet by Jennifer A. McGowan
ISBN: 978-1-909208-35-3
Narrative poems based in myth and folk stories from around the world.
Happy Ending NOT Guaranteed by Liam Hogan
ISBN: 978-1-909208-36-0
Deliciously twisted fantasy stories.

BACK LIST:

Short Stories

London Lies
ISBN: 978-1-909208-00-1
Our first Liars' League showcase, featuring unlikely tales set in London.
Stations: Short Stories Inspired by the Overground line
ISBN: 978-1-909208-01-8
A story for every station from New Cross, Crystal Palace, and West Croydon at the Southern extremes of the East London branch of the Overground line, all the way to Highbury & Islington.
Lovers' Lies
ISBN: 978-1-909208-02-5
Our second collaboration with Liars' League, bringing the freshness, wit, imagination and passion of their authors to stories of love.

Weird Lies
ISBN: 978-1-909208-10-0
WINNER of the Saboteur2014 Best Anthology Award: our
third Liars' League collaboration – more than twenty stories
varying in style from tales not out of place in *One Thousand and
One Nights* to the completely bemusing.
Solstice Shorts: Sixteen Stories about Time
ISBN: 978-1-909208-23-0
Winning stories from the first *Solstice Shorts Festival* competition
together with a story from each of the competition judges.
Mosaic of Air by Cherry Potts
ISBN: 978-1-909208-03-2
Sixteen short stories from a lesbian perspective.
Liberty Tales, Stories & Poems inspired by Magna Carta edited by
Cherry Potts
ISBN: 978-1-909208-31-5
Because freedom is never out of fashion.

Poetry

The Other Side of Sleep: Narrative Poems
ISBN: 978-1-909208-18-6
Long, narrative poems by contemporary voices, including Inua
Elams, Brian Johnstone, and Kate Foley, whose title poem for
the anthology was the winner of the 2014 *Second Light* Long
Poem competition.
The Don't Touch Garden by Kate Foley
ISBN: 978-1-909208-19-3
A complex autobiographical collection of poems of adoption
and identity, from award-winning poet Kate Foley.

Novels

Devilskein & Dearlove by Alex Smith
ISBN: 978-1-909208-15-5
NOMINATED FOR THE 2015 CILIP CARNEGIE MEDAL.
A young adult novel set in South Africa. Young Erin Dearlove has lost everything, and is living in a run-down apartment block in Cape Town. Then she has tea with Mr Devilskein, the demon who lives on the top floor, and opens a door into another world.

The Dowry Blade by Cherry Potts
ISBN: 979-1-909208-20-9
When nomad Brede finds a wounded mercenary and the Dowry Blade, she is set on a journey of revenge, love, and loss.

Photography

Outcome: LGBT Portraits by Tom Dingley
ISBN: 978-1-909208-26-1
80 full colour photographic portraits of LGBT people with the attributes of their daily life – and a photograph of themselves as a child. @OutcomeLGBT

All our books (except *The Other Side of Sleep* and *The Don't Touch Garden)* are also available as e-books.

EVENTS

Arachne Press is enthusiastic about live literature and we make an effort to present our books through readings.

The Solstice Shorts Festival
(http://arachnepress.com/solstice-shorts)
Now in its third year, Solstice Shorts is all about time: held on the shortest day of the year on the Prime meridian, stories, poetry and song celebrate the turning of the moon, the changing of the seasons, the motions of the spheres, and clockwork!

This year's shortest day theme was made more complex by asking authors and musicians to respond to each other and we are very grateful to Lester Simpson for teaching us the traditional songs and Zachary Gvirtzman for the three pieces he provided, *Still Ill, Two Blind Elephants*, and *Sonata for Two Violins* and which informed so much of the writing – see if you can spot which! – and to Juliet Desailly for her song, based on Joan Leotta's poem.

We showcase our work and that of others at our own bi-monthly live literature event, in south London: *The Story Sessions,* which we run like a folk club, with headliners and opportunities for the audience to join in (http://arachnepress.com/the-story-sessions) We are always on the lookout for other places to show off, so if you run a bookshop, a literature festival or any other kind of literature venue, get in touch; we'd love to talk to you.

WORKSHOPS

We offer writing workshops suitable for writers' groups, literature festivals and evening classes, which are sometimes supported by live music – if you are interested, please get in touch.